December Kiss

The Snowberry Series Book 2

Katie Mettner

ISBN-10 : 1500540676
ISBN-13 : 978-1500540678

Cover design by: Carrie Butler
Printed in the United States of America

Dear Reader,

When you first meet Snow and Jay, I'm sure you'll be surprised by the complicated wheelchairs they use in this story. Most readers think they aren't real. This is fiction, after all, right? The truth is, there is a real prototype of this chair undergoing tests and trials as we speak. It started in a guy's garage made from a lawn chair, a motor and wheels, to a fully functional voice recognition wheelchair. The technology was already at our fingertips to bring a chair like this to the market, so it makes sense this is the next step. I hope one day I can sit in one of these chairs and say, "Forward, hands" and be able to hold hands with my husband while my wheelchair does the work. I want you to know that I strive to make my stories as realistic as I can because you, the reader, deserve that. While the chair is not on the market yet, I enjoyed writing a story based on the idea that one day it will be, and it will change the lives of so many people!

Be well,

Katie

Dedication:

To Tobi and Stephanie, because without their encouragement, Jay's story wouldn't exist.

Chapter One

There was a subtle snick of air leaking from somewhere, and then my chair slowly came to a halt. Great, just what I need. *What a bright idea to wheel to lunch, Jay, bright idea.* This wheelchair was about to find itself a new home … in a dumpster. I sighed, if only I could afford a new one. I dug in the bag under my legs, praying for a new inner tube. I stuck the small portable air pump next to my leg and kept digging, but came up empty-handed. I had the air pump and the tools to change the tube, but no tube. Swell.

I gazed up at the clear blue sky. It was almost noon and the sun shone heavy on my back, leaving a trickle of sweat under my suit coat to pool at the base of my spine. It might be November in Minnesota, but someone forgot to tell Mother Nature. I wiped my forehead with the sleeve of my coat and weighed my options. I could call Dad and have him pick me up on his lunch break, or sit here and wait for someone to come along and rescue this *damsel in distress*. I glanced around the deserted town square and frowned.

Dad it is.

I bumped the chair along toward a bench farther away from the street, praying I didn't damage the rim or the tire. I scooted onto a park bench to avoid any more pressure on the expensive titanium rims before I called for help. Not that it mattered. The chair was so old and so beat up nothing short of running it over with my truck could do much more damage.

Having been unemployed since I graduated from college in June, I wasn't flush enough to buy a new one. Sure, I had some money saved, but a new wheelchair would be close to four grand, and that would wipe out my savings. That's why today's interview was imperative. It was the one interview I'd been praying for. I thought it went well, and, as far as I could tell, I stood as good of a chance as anyone.

To celebrate, I thought it was a great idea to enjoy the rest of the day with fish and chips at Buck's Tackle Barn, but I should have known better. Nothing is ever a great idea if I have to count on this chair. I slipped my suit coat off and laid it on the wheelchair then leaned back on the bench and tried to stretch out my back. I needed to land this job, so I could get on with my life. I'm grateful to my brother, Dully, for letting me stay with them, but I couldn't mooch off them forever.

"Is everything alright?" a voice asked and I glanced up from my phone into a beautiful pair of amber eyes.

I was silent for a moment as I lost myself in

them, then shook my head a little, nodding slowly. "Yeah, sorry, you surprised me." I smiled and stuck my hand out. "I'm Jay."

She reached forward and grasped my hand, her skin soft and warm. "I'm December. It's nice to meet you, Jay." She pointed at my chair, which was now tilting dangerously to the left. "Looks like you've run aground sailor."

I made a sound that was lacking in mirth while I loosened my tie. "I'm afraid I miscalculated the tire pressure."

She inspected the chair and the wheel, lifting up on the left side and letting the tire spin. In less than one rotation, she set it back down and picked at it, triumphantly holding up a roofing nail. "Looks like you're a victim of Alan's Construction."

I lowered my head to my hands and ran my fingers through my hair. Great, now I had a hole in the tube and the tire. I'd be spending the rest of my night repairing the chair again. It was time to get a loan from the Bank of Alexander and hit eBay for a *new-to-me* chair.

I realized December was still standing there holding the nail, and I made eye contact again. "Thanks for finding that. I, uh, didn't think to check. I pop those darn tubes all the time."

She pocketed the nail and smiled. "It's no problem. I'd be happy to give you a ride somewhere if you need it. I'm just heading to work."

I let my eyes travel the length of her, taking in the light green scrubs with *Providence Hospital* printed on the pocket.

"You work at the hospital?" I asked and she nodded.

"Yup. I'm an RN in the recovery room, but occasionally I work in the ER. You look familiar, do you work there?"

"Not yet, but I just left an interview there, so cross your fingers. You might know my sister-in-law, Snow Alexander?"

"No way! You're Dully's little brother?"

I held my hands out and shrugged, "That's me."

The recognition played across her face and she nodded, but the smile stayed in place. "Snow talks about you nonstop, but she calls you Jason."

"That's my real name, but I hate it. I go by Jay, but Snow hasn't warmed up to the idea," I admitted, laughing a little uncomfortably.

She pulled a key from her pocket. "Stay here, I was just heading to my car, which is parked over there." She pointed, and my eyes followed her finger. It was an SUV of some sort, which meant my chair would fit in it no problem. "I'll pull it up and give you a ride to wherever you need to go."

I sighed, as much as I hated to take her up on her offer, she was going to the hospital. "I'd appreciate a ride back to the hospital. My truck is there."

She clapped twice. "It was a sign then! Stay put, I'll be right back."

I wiggled my brows toward the chair. "I'm not going anywhere."

She smacked herself in the forehead with her

palm. "No, I guess you aren't. Well, at least not in that chair, but I know you're going places. Snow told me so."

She winked and then jogged off toward the green SUV. Her honey brown hair was held at the nape of her neck in a ponytail and waved against her shoulders as she ran. My eyes focused on her backside, and hard as I tried not to, I couldn't help but notice she filled out those scrubs like no other nurse I'd ever seen. I rolled my eyes a little and picked up my coat. *Mind out of the gutter, Jay.* My buddies used to ogle girls constantly in college, and I'd be the one to tell them to have some respect. Now here I am ogling the woman coming to save my sorry butt from roasting to death in the sun.

I waited while she pulled around the block before I transferred back into my chair, then ker-thunked to the curb. She parked and came around the Jeep to open the passenger door. It was then that I saw the problem. The chair was too low for me to get up into the seat of the SUV. I was instantly embarrassed, which was a pretty common occurrence in my life. While my upper body strength made me arm wrestling champion of my dorm, if I didn't have anything to pull myself up with, I wasn't going anywhere.

"This isn't going to work," I said, but she pulled the back door open and reappeared with a patient transfer belt. She looped one through the grab bar near the door.

"Sure it will. Grab the belt, and I'll guide you in," she encouraged me. Even if I was extremely uncomfortable being this intimate with a stranger, I couldn't bring myself to be rude and tell her no. I grabbed the belt and hauled myself up from the chair, while she slid one arm under my knees and lifted me into the seat. "See? Piece of cake. Let me put the chair in the back hatch and we'll be on our way."

I nodded mutely and she shut the door, opening the hatch to store my chair. I leaned my head back on the seat and banged it a couple of times. On days like this I really hated being in a chair. The one time I meet a cute girl she has to help my handicapped butt. Check another one off the list of *Don't even stand a chance of getting a date* list. I half-snorted. Not that I ever stood a chance at getting a date with her or anyone else for that matter. The chair was always a visible barrier for most women, even more so when it was broken down.

I punched my fist into my knee and took a deep breath, reminding myself that getting angry wouldn't solve anything. Accept the ride, thank her, and go home. Tomorrow is a new day.

She slid into her seat and put the shifter into drive, signaling as she pulled left into traffic. "I feel like I know so much about you just by what Snow has told me. You just graduated from college, right?"

"Yeah, well, in June. I have a degree in social work," I said, making small talk. The hospital was only a few blocks away and soon I could escape this awkward situation and be done with this day.

"Providence is hiring a social worker. Our last one left for a bigger hospital."

I motioned to the suit. "Cue Jay Alexander from the left," I said in my best director's voice. She half-snorted, half-laughed and I chuckled. "That's why my truck is at the hospital. I just left the interview. I was going to have lunch, but …" I motioned to the back of the car and she smiled.

"I hope you get the job. We need fresh blood in that department. You strike me as the kind of guy who doesn't get rattled easily."

I laughed then, an honest to goodness *that was funny* kind of laugh. "I'd like to say that's true, but right now I'm sitting in a car with a beautiful woman, forgive me for saying so, and cursing that wheelchair because once again I had to succumb to help from said beautiful woman. I'm actually quite rattled, but over the years I've learned to hide it well."

She turned right into the hospital parking lot and slowed at the entrance. Her face lit up with a smile and she patted my knee. "I won't forgive you for saying I'm a beautiful woman. In fact, I'll say thank you. It's nice to hear a compliment once in a while from a guy who isn't telling me that because he wants me to give him pain meds."

I laughed again and shook my head. She was delightful. What a shame we had to meet the way we did. "I bet you get buttered up a lot."

She gave me the so-so hand. "If you call three times an hour a lot. I hope you'll forgive me for taking charge and stepping in, but I like to help. It's kind of what I do." She pulled her SUV up next to my truck and put the car in park.

"How did you know that's my truck?" I asked and she put her finger to her lips and tapped it.

"Well, it's parked in handicapped, it's a low-rider, and it has a wheelchair lift in the bed. I might have just graduated from college, but I can put two and two together." She winked and I blushed. It wasn't from embarrassment, though. It was from something else I couldn't explain.

"Of course, see, like I said, I get rattled easily. You just graduated, too?"

We unbuckled our belts at the same time and she turned to me. "Last December from nursing school. I started working here in February when I was recruited from Rochester. Everyone thought I was crazy for leaving Mayo Clinic, but I wanted to work in a smaller hospital. So, anyway, let me grab your chair."

She jumped from the car and pulled open the hatch. I turned in the seat and watched her strong arms pull the chair down, and carefully set it on the wheels.

She stuck her head in the back. "Hey, how are you going to get this fixed? Do you need me to call Snow?"

"I have a repair kit in my truck. I'll pull the wheel off and fix it before I leave," I said and she nodded before closing the hatch.

I watched in the mirror as she rolled the chair forward on the front two wheels and then set it next to the door. I opened it and we repeated the earlier process to get back into the chair. I clicked open the lock on my truck and pulled open the driver's side door.

"Thanks for the ride back. I hope I didn't make you late," I stuttered.

"Nah, my boss is cool. I sent her a text to let her know I'd be a few minutes late," December said, standing on the running board of her Jeep. "I gotta move this to employee parking. Are you sure you'll be okay?"

I smiled up at her and nodded. "I'm good, thanks again. Hey, I'd like to make it up to you. Can I buy you dinner sometime?"

"I'd like that. I'm new to town and don't know too many people. I'd really like to get to know you better, Jay. I'm off Friday and Saturday." She smiled and waited. I was smiling at her in disbelief that she had actually accepted my invitation.

I realized she was waiting for an answer and I stuttered about a little before I could form a sentence. "Say, ah, Saturday would be great. I have to take Sunny to gymnastics in the morning, but I'm free after that. How about four o'clock?"

"Perfect! I gotta go, but I'll get your number from Snow and text you directions?"

I nodded and she waved, ready to climb in when I called her name. "December, wait, what's your last name?" I asked and she popped her head back out, a naughty grin tipping her lips.

"Kiss."

And then she was gone.

Chapter Two

"Sunny, stay over here, Mommy will be home soon," I called to my four-year-old niece who was bouncing her ball near the driveway. It was Friday and I'd offered to let her stay home from daycare today, so we could spend the day together. Dully was running late at school, but Snow would be home any minute. I was on the deck in my now repaired chair, researching on the laptop, and sipping a Diet Coke.

I watched Sunny climb up the ramp and wiggle up onto a chaise lounge next to me. She leaned against the back and crossed her ankles, her legs barely reaching the middle of the cushion. One look at the sprite and no one would ever question who her mother is. She was the tiny porcelain doll of her mother, from the snow-white hair to the pink lipped smile and tiny features. She was beautiful in a tiny little girl way, but I knew when she grew up, she'd be stunning. Take one look in her eyes though, and you also knew she was an Alexander. Her eyes were exactly the same as her fathers, and equally as disturbing and compelling, one grey and one green.

When they laid this babe in my arms the first time, I was a goner. I might have been a twenty-something college kid, but I instantly became a big blubbering idiot holding her on that bright August day. She was almost a month early, deciding she wanted to make an entrance when none of us were expecting it. I was lucky to be home for the summer still and was one of the first to hold her and rock her to sleep. My fate was sealed that day and now I'm the biggest pushover uncle ever.

Maybe we have a special connection because I'm the one who chose her name. Okay, not technically, but it was my idea. Snow was joking one day about how growing up with a name like Snow was fun. Even though sometimes it was annoying, especially when your last name was Daze, it was fun to have a name no one else had. After they found out she was having a girl, they argued for months about names. At dinner one night I said, *I think you should name her Sunshine and we can call her Sunny*. I was joking, but the day she was born, Snow and Dully took one look at her and declared her name Sunshine Rose Alexander. That day, August twenty-first, changed my life. It was the day I finally figured out what I wanted to do with my life.

When I left for college, I was convinced I could never do anything successfully. I was an aimless kid who had a chip on his shoulder about all the things he couldn't do. I couldn't walk, run, or dance. I didn't even want to go to college, but Dully insisted, saying I'd discover new things about myself there.

I hated to admit that he was right. College was hard work and not a lot of fun most of the time, but I learned a few things about myself there. They weren't the important things, though. That happened when I held a little five-pound baby girl in my arms. I went back to school a few weeks after she was born and changed my major to social work. On the weekends, I came home and spent every spare minute I had with Sunny, watching her grow while she taught me how to let a lot of things go. I guess you could say we grew up together. She might only be four, but in those four years, I learned how to care about something other than myself.

I was probably also living vicariously through my brother. I may never have a family of my own, and I didn't want to miss out on a second of her childhood. I glanced over and she was rubbing her hands on the smooth wood arms and smiling up at me.

"Uncle Jay, can we go down to the pond?" she asked sweetly.

I sighed, hating to disappoint her. "Not today, baby, Uncle Jay's chair hasn't been behaving," I tried to explain in a way she understood.

Her shoulders slumped and she frowned. "I'll push you if you get stuck, I promise," she begged.

"Sunny, I said no. Not today," I said sharply and instantly saw the hurt in her eyes.

"I'm going to my room," she grumped, climbing off the lounger.

"Sweetheart, I'm sorry. Come sit on my lap," I said, but she shook her head and stormed through the patio doors. "Sunny, come here," I called and waited for her to poke her head back out, but she didn't.

I pounded the table with my fist and my soda can jumped, a few drops spilling over the side. "Man, you are stressed out," I muttered.

"About what, dear?" a voice asked and I jumped, my hand slamming the laptop closed as my mom walked up the ramp.

"Oh, hi, Mom," I greeted her, kissing her cheek when she bent down to hug me.

"Hi. Dully said you have Sweet Pea. Where is she?" Mom asked, looking around the yard.

"She's in her room," I sighed. "Maybe if you call her she will come down."

"She doesn't want to come down?" she asked, surprised.

I picked imaginary lint off my shorts so I didn't have to make eye contact. "She's a little upset with me. She wanted to go to the pond and I told her no."

The patio doors slid open and her little head bobbed out. She came over to me and crawled up on my lap, putting her arms around my neck.

"I'm sorry for not listening, Uncle Jay, and I'm sorry your chair is being a pain. Can I go play in the sandbox?"

I squeezed her tightly for a moment. "You're okay, sweetheart. I'm sorry for being crabby. Go play. Daddy will be home soon." I kissed her cheek and she skipped down the ramp to her sandbox near the deck.

"Your chair is being a pain?" Mom asked when Sunny was out of earshot.

"When isn't it?" I asked and she gave me her mom eyebrow. The one that always made me feel guilty for talking smartly to her. "I'm a little stressed out. I'm sorry for talking back," I apologized and she patted my back.

"Your chair is falling apart, Jay. Dad and I want to buy you a new one. We're afraid it's going to leave you stranded one day."

I barked with laughter and her other brow went up. "That was yesterday, after my interview." I shook my head at the memory. "I ran over a nail and it took out the tube and the tire. Luckily, a nurse from the hospital came upon my broken down butt and drove me back to my truck." I opened my laptop and turned it toward her. "I've been looking on eBay, but can't find one my size. I can't afford to buy a new one out of pocket right now. I have the last payment from my modeling contract, but I might need that if I can't find a job around here. I know you and Dad can't afford a new one either."

She sighed and shook her head. "Jay, we can afford to get you a new chair. We've been saving since you got this one. I wish you had told us sooner, you have enough to deal with, and you need a safe chair."

I glanced up, surprised by that information. "I didn't know. I don't like to ask, but I can't find a job if my chair keeps breaking down. I'm kind of stressed and don't know where to turn."

I heard tires on the blacktop and Snow rolled to a stop in the driveway. She lowered the side door of her van and rolled out in MAC, where she was greeted by her smiling daughter yelling, *mommy, mommy*. Sunny was no sooner on her mother's lap than my brother pulled his Dodge Magnum behind Snow's van. I was secretly glad they were both home. I needed to decompress with a beer and my bed.

Snow rode with Sunny up the ramp to where mom and I sat, with Dully right behind them. Sunny was chatting a mile a minute about everything we'd done today. Mom stood and pulled Sunny off Snow's lap, and then hugged Dully, before distracting her granddaughter with sidewalk chalk.

"Sounds like you had a busy day," Snow said, laughing. Dully pulled out a chair and straddled it to chat with me.

"We did everything from having a tea party to jumping rope. Well, she jumped and I watched." I rolled my eyes and Dully snorted.

"Except you didn't go to the pond because your chair was not behaving," Snow parroted, one brow raised and I half-nodded, half-shrugged.

"Nothing new there. It's working again, but I didn't want to go to the pond and get stuck when I was here alone with her. I didn't mean to upset her."

Dully shook his head. "Don't let it bother you. Kids need to understand that sometimes we do things to protect them. That's all you were doing. She's fine." He pointed at where she was drawing a hopscotch grid on the driveway.

"I was just telling Jason he needs to let us buy him a new chair. This one is beyond repair and we're worried about him getting hurt," Mom told Dully, and both he and Snow agreed.

"After yesterday, I couldn't agree more, Mom. Even though I'm secretly thrilled that chair took a dump right where December could happen upon him, he certainly can't go pick her up for their date in that chair," Snow said, grinning.

I crossed my arms over my chest, my biceps bulging. "It's not a date. It's just dinner," I informed her.

"Right, a dinner date." She smirked and I rolled my eyes at her. The woman was a matchmaking maniac.

"Well, unless you're going to loan me MAC, I'm picking her up in this. It will take a few weeks to get a new chair." I turned to Mom, who was leaning on the edge of the railing. "I'll accept a loan for the chair, but once I get a job, I want to pay you back."

Mom was about to object when Snow chimed in. "I can't loan you MAC, because I'm not riding around in that piece of titanium crap, but I have something better." She motioned for us to follow her and we rolled down the ramp one after the other. We stopped at her van and she hit the latch button for the back. It swung open and sitting in the back was a new chair. Dully lifted it down, wearing a big old grin, which told me he knew what was going on here.

"Jay, meet Sport. The newest prototype in MAC chairs." Snow motioned at the chair like Vanna White. It was nearly identical to hers.

"What the …" I couldn't form a sentence, so I just wheeled my chair a little closer, and took in the beauty that was Sport. "I didn't know you had a new prototype."

"That's because we weren't sure how long it would take us to get it ready for market. We've been working on it since, let's see, since Liam met you."

I turned my chair to gaze at her. "Dr. Liam James?"

She nodded. "One and the same. The day he met you, he decided we needed a chair made specifically for guys who would benefit from all the features of MAC, and added features for sporting activities. Essentially, Sport has the capability to change wheels quickly to any camber angle without changing the tubes. It also comes with all-terrain, road, and court tires that change out quickly and easily with no tools. Sport weighs a little bit more than MAC but can get wet for short periods, say for duck hunting. You can still fold it with the touch of a button, and he fits in the front seat of a car," she finished proudly.

I sat with my mouth hanging open, trying to force words through my lips. "Snow, that's totally sci-fi in the disabled world. People have multiple wheelchairs to do what you just described," I stuttered.

"I know, that's why I agreed to work with Liam on this. Why have three chairs when you can have one? MAC Sport will be more expensive, but you won't need an everyday chair, a sport chair, and a water chair. Plus, you get the added benefit of hands-free control, and whether you're playing basketball or tennis, it will certainly give you an advantage. Don't just sit there, get in it." She pointed and I shook my head.

"I don't want to break it," I admitted, a little intimidated by the description she gave me. There's high-tech and then there's high-tech in Snow's world.

"Jason, do you get what she's saying?" Dully asked, laying his hand on my shoulder. I stared up at him, my eyes answering the question for him. "Liam built this chair for you. He wants you to use it and see if you can break it. Sport is your chair."

I glanced at Snow and then back to Dully and back to Snow, who was nodding now. "Liam says the guy who inspired it should ride it. If you decide you want to test drive Sport, you'll have to come into the research lab every so often for adjustments, and we'll need to pull data from the chair. Of course, we also need feedback from you. Our only other stipulation is that you don't divulge anything about the chair, other than calling it Sport. Patent is pending on it and we don't want the idea stolen before we get it to market. Not that anyone could, since it's taken us three years to develop this technology, but better safe than sorry."

"Snow, I don't know what to say." I wheeled around the back of the chair, inspecting it from every angle. It looked a lot like hers, but it said *Sport* on the back and the undercarriage was different.

"Say you'll try it out, for heaven's sake!" my mom exclaimed from the driveway and we all started laughing.

I locked my chair and swung myself across into its seat. The memory foam seat molded itself to me almost instantly and my spine relaxed, the pressure from my weight sitting on my spinal malformation dissipating. It was something I'd had to get used to over the years, but suddenly the ache eased a little. I closed my eyes and swallowed, noticing Dully's hands on my shoulders.

"How does it feel?" Snow whispered.

I couldn't open my eyes and look at her for fear I'd sob. "The pain in my back was gone almost instantly," I said through a choked voice.

She clapped once and I opened my eyes to gaze into her teary ones. "There's a new gel pad memory foam design on it. I had it made to relieve all the pressure points on your spine. I'll apologize ahead of time for breaking protocol and pulling your medical records to get the info, but you did give us medical power of attorney." She smiled and I shook my head, trying not to cry like a baby.

"Nothing to forgive, you can't even imagine how I'm feeling right now." I stopped and then hit myself in the forehead. "Well, maybe you can, but you know what I mean."

"It's a lot to take in, but I knew you were the right guy for the job. Speaking of jobs, Lars handed me this on the way out the door and asked me to deliver it," she said, pulling an envelope from MAC.

I looked at the envelope and in the corner was the letterhead from Providence Hospital. It had only been yesterday that I'd interviewed. "Wow, guess the denials come quickly around here." I tapped the envelope on my knee but made no move to open it.

Snow pointed at it. "May I?"

I nodded, and she tore it open, reading it aloud. *"Dear Jay, it was wonderful to meet you, blah, blah. We think you would bring a unique point of view to the social worker position here, blah, blah. We would like to extend the offer for the position, blah, blah."*

I snatched the letter from her hand, her face shining with happiness. Dully was leaning over my shoulder, reading the letter with me. I read it top to bottom and then, for good measure, read it again.

"I got the job?" I asked in disbelief.

"You got the job!" Snow sang happily. "All of us there hope you accept it because you're perfect for the job, Jay." Snow grinned and I leaned forward and kissed her cheek.

"Did you have anything to do with this?" I asked, holding up the letter.

She shook her head and patted my face. "No, I didn't need to put my two cents in, nor would I. You got the job all on your own. They were impressed with who you are, not just as a social worker, but as a person. They had no idea little Jason Alexander had come back to town with a degree in social work."

Sunny climbed up on my lap. "Are you gonna take the job, Uncle Jay? I want you to stay here and live with us forever."

I put my arm around her and squeezed her to my side. "I'd be kind of crazy not to take the job, right?" I asked and everyone's head bobbed. My mom was crying and I definitely could start at any moment.

"I got the job," I said aloud again. "I can't believe I got the job."

Snow rubbed my arm tenderly. "I think you should go call them, don't you?"

"Yes. Yes, I should. Thank you for bringing this home, Snow. I'm going to call them and accept the position," I rambled. "Also, thank you for Sport. You just lifted forty tons off my shoulders with this chair. Mom and Dad's, too. Man, I'm all out of words except thank you."

Snow smiled and winked. "You don't need words. I can look at your shoulders and see that the forty tons are gone. You're about to live your dreams and I'm glad Sport was ready at the perfect time. He'll take you places, as long as you trust your heart."

I nodded, my chin wobbling at her confidence in me.

Dully patted my shoulder. "I'm proud of you, Jay. I'm so proud of everything you are. Congratulations, no one deserves this more than you."

I glanced up from my chair into his smiling face and remembered a time when he wasn't so proud of me. I vowed never to disappoint him that way again.

Chapter Three

"You don't clean up half bad, Jay," I muttered at my reflection as I straightened my tie in the mirror. It was Saturday and only a little after two, but I had to stop and pick up some flowers. Tonight was my date with December.

"A thank-you dinner, Jay. It's not a date. Don't let Snow feed you unrealistic expectations," I scolded the face in the mirror.

Feeling like an idiot for talking to myself, I wheeled my chair back out to the front room and grabbed my wallet off the table. If I had to pick her up across town by four, I had better leave in a few minutes to stop at Savannah's. It always takes me longer than the average guy to do the basic things. I swallowed nervously. Dating women who weren't in a wheelchair was always intimidating. I don't want to hold them up or make them impatient or uncomfortable.

"It's not a date, man. It's just dinner to say thanks for saving your sorry butt," I recited aloud again. I'd been trying to convince myself it wasn't a date all day, but it sure felt like one. It was probably just Snow's subliminal messaging at work.

I tucked the wallet into the side pocket of Sport and grabbed my suit coat, shrugging into it. The past week had been warm, but today the temperature had dropped almost thirty degrees.

Last night, we enjoyed the unnaturally warm November air and grilled pork chops on the deck. After dinner, Snow and I spent a good deal of time going over the ins and outs of how Sport was programmed. To say it was intense was an understatement, but it didn't take me long to get the hang of it.

Now, I can make Sport do anything I need it to with simple commands. It helped that I'd been watching Snow run MAC for the last four years, but I was surprised at the built-in features Sport has that even MAC doesn't have. At first, I felt silly talking to the chair and my voice was stiff and unnatural. The chair wouldn't run until I relaxed and spoke to it in my normal voice.

I found it weird at first until Snow informed me she had recorded conversations we'd had over the last few months to teach the chair my voice intonation. Since Sport only knew my voice in certain cadences, I had to speak the same way for him to recognize it was me. It was seriously sci-fi stuff. I can push Sport manually like any other chair, but it detects only my voice in a room full of people if I give it a command. I guess it would be a little hard if it picked up other people's voices and started doing odd things during a party. I snickered a little and rolled to the couch.

This morning, I distracted myself with some last-minute winterizing around the cabin with Dully, including getting the fireplace ready for the winter. I had lived in Dully and Snow's small two-bedroom cabin near the pond since I graduated. It was where I would stay on the weekends and during summer break when I was in college. It was completely handicapped accessible and made my life very easy. I hated how hard it was going to be to leave the little cabin, and the safety of my family, but I would have to find a new place to live. Now that I had a job, I couldn't continue to monopolize their guest house.

When I promised Dully this morning to be out by the first of the year, he made me promise not to talk about leaving just yet. He said since Snow doesn't have any family and our parents live across the pond, they don't have a pressing need for a guest house right now. It was a little bit of a relief and I agreed to stay until spring when moving would be easier. Monday, I would put my name on the list for the handicapped condos where Snow used to live. There wasn't much housing in this town that was new and met ADA guidelines. The majority of the rentals were apartments plenty of stairs, which was definitely not going to work for me.

I slid over onto the couch, pulling my legs up to tie my shoes. I rested my elbow on my knees and glanced around the room. The wooden logs weren't but a few years old, and already looked weathered and worn. The living room was huge, with a fireplace that stretched to the ceiling in the middle of the room, leaving open areas on each side. The kitchen had state of the art appliances and a small table in the middle of the room. My bedroom and bathroom were as open and airy as the living room and kitchen, which made my life easy when it came to cleaning up and dressing.

My favorite part of the cabin was the fireplace, though. I'd spent hours sitting in front of it, reading a book, studying, or playing with Sunny. It was the way I liked to heat the cabin in the winter because it made me feel like I was out in the woods, living in the wilderness. I slid back into Sport and patted the sides.

Now that I had this chair, maybe I could go out into the wilderness and experience it without needing Dully to do all the work. He never seemed to mind, but now that he's getting older and has a family, I wouldn't want him to get hurt trying to help me. He's helped me enough over the past twenty-some years. It was time to stand on my own two feet. Not literally, of course. I've never been able to stand on my own two feet, but figuratively for sure. Starting this new job in my hometown was just the beginning. Staying in my hometown and being near Sunny and my family was more than I could ask for. I was definitely feeling the blessings the last week had offered me. First, I met December, then I got my dream job and a dream wheelchair. I was flying high for the first time in a long time.

I picked the coat up off the rack and laid it on my lap then rolled down the ramp from the cabin. The afternoon sun was already waning in the sky as Thanksgiving approached. I wasn't surprised to see Dully leaning against the side. We had always been attuned to each other and he knew I was freaking out right about now. I stopped the chair in front of the passenger side door and he nodded his head in approval.

"I like the way you clean up, little brother. I think December will, too." He grinned and I punched him in the gut.

He let out a small puff of air but didn't double over, having already braced for what he knew was coming. When you grow up with a brother in a wheelchair, you pretty much expect to get punched in the gut every time.

"You're a real comedian today, brother. Tell me again why you're holding up my truck?" I asked, pulling the cold metal door of the handle and yanking the door open.

"My wife," he answered and I had to bite the inside of my cheek to keep from laughing.

"Why didn't your wife come if she was so concerned?" I asked, hoisting myself onto the seat before bending to lift my legs in.

Dully never moved off the side of the truck, just turned his body to face me. "She's busy with Sunny. She just wanted to make sure you didn't have any problems folding Sport and getting him in the truck."

I never took my eyes off him, reaching my finger out and pushing the red button on the side of the chair until it folded. I compressed the wheel pins and lifted them across my chest into the front of the truck, then I lifted Sport and did the same. When I was finished, I popped my head out of the now open window.

"Ta-da!" I cracked and he rolled his eyes. "I've been doing this for a lot of years, but tell your wife thanks for the concern. Chances are she sent you down here to make sure I wasn't going on my *date*," which I put in air quotes, "in jeans and a sweatshirt."

He smiled a naughty smile and stuck his hands in his pockets. "You know that woman almost as well as I do. Almost. Now, call me if you need anything or if Sport stops cooperating. Otherwise, have fun." He leaned down into the window and looked me straight in the eye. "Remember, no one else can define your self-worth. As long as you stay true to who you are, she will love spending the evening with you."

I gave an almost imperceptible nod and started the truck. He stepped back and held up one hand in a wave. I gave him the same motion and remembered back to the time I thought it would be our last.

KISS

"Can I help you find something?" a voice asked, and I turned Sport, knowing what was coming.

"You always do." I grinned and was rewarded with a bear hug of epic proportions.

"Jay! What are you doing here?" Savannah exclaimed, leaning back and wiping her hands on her apron. Today's selection was of giraffes running across the African plains.

I glanced around the flower shop for a moment. "I'm here to buy flowers. From what I hear, this is the place to do it."

She giggled happily and then walked around me, doing a full three-sixty. "Well, no wonder I didn't recognize you. Between the suit and the chair, you don't look like the scruffy college kid I used to know."

"I'm afraid that scruffy college kid is no more. You're looking at the newest social worker at Providence Hospital." I grinned and she squealed. She jumped up and down and then hugged me again.

"Jay, I'm so happy for you! Dully and Snow must be over the moon."

"They are, and so is Sunny. Snow came home yesterday with this new chair for me, and the letter offering the job. The suit, well, that's all me, baby." I winked.

Savannah walked around the chair and whistled. "Sport, huh? This looks awfully suspicious of my bestie's handiwork."

I patted the wheels. "Some of hers and some of

Dr. James, but together they asked me to take Sport for a test drive. I've had it for about eighteen hours, and I already don't want to give it back."

"Is it like MAC?" she asked excitedly and I laid my finger against my lips.

"I'm not allowed to talk about it..." I whispered conspiratorially.

"Or you'd have to kill me?" she asked shocked and I gave her the palms up.

"I'd never do that, but Snow might whip me with a wet noodle, so I better mind my Ps and Qs. Speaking of which, I need some flowers."

"What's the occasion, Jay?" she asked, walking to the cooler and pausing with her hand on the door.

"*Thank you for rescuing my sorry butt when my tire got a nail in it and I didn't have a spare with me* occasion," I reeled off without blinking.

She started to snicker and soon was laughing as though thoroughly tickled. "That sounds like a totally sucky day for you! Well, maybe not that sucky. How cute is she?"

"Let's just say she's easy on the eyes. Maybe you know her. December Kiss?" I asked and her eyes went wide.

"I know of her, and she's gorgeous. She works out at the hospital gym. I've been there with Snow before. You lucky dog, you."

She stood staring at me and I was about to open my mouth when she clapped her hands again and spun on her heel.

"I have just the thing! Stay here," she exclaimed, running from the room.

I laughed into the empty room because that was Savannah at her finest. When I first met Snow's best friend, I was a little taken aback. She was always in hyper mode and rarely took a breath before moving on to the next subject. As time passed, and we got together more often, I began to see it wasn't that she was hyper, she just enjoyed life that much. She had no time for negativity but would help anyone at the drop of a hat. She even offered me a job when I graduated from college, but I declined. I would have been a bull in a flower shop and cost her money.

When I told her that, she frowned, then tried to talk me into sitting by the counter and flexing my muscles. She said word would travel that she had the best flowers and the hottest helpers in town, and business would boom. Every so often, I come by and sit next to her counter, flexing my muscles for fun.

She ran back into the room and laid a paper on the counter, then began gathering flowers and greens from the cooler. She ducked back behind the counter, laying the flowers and greens out, snipping stems and humming as she worked.

"December Kiss. That's such a great name. Almost as good as Snow Daze. Did she really rescue you from a flat tire on your truck?"

I laughed then, long and silly as she stared at me like I was a crazy man. "The flat wasn't on my truck."

"Oh, no! Not that piece of dirt chair again?" Savannah threw the flower she was holding down and put one hand on her hip.

"I'm afraid so. It dumped my butt on the way to Buck's, and I was lucky December came along. She was heading to work and was able to give me a lift back to my truck. It was still at the hospital from my interview." I patted Sport. "But that problem is solved. Tonight, I can pick her up in Sport and not give a second thought to a breakdown."

Savannah went back to work on the flowers and tried to raise her right brow, but failed. "I'm sorry, Jay, I know that chair was really bad. I'm glad Snow brought you Sport. We were all getting worried. It looks like it may have worked out in your favor, though." She rolled the paper and wound a ribbon around it. It was a ribbon covered with red lipstick kisses.

"Savannah, how's your eye?" I asked, hoping to catch her off guard.

Her hand went directly to her right eye and she refused to meet mine. "It's fine."

It wasn't fine, though. Since I'd come back from college in June, it was getting worse. Her right eye didn't move the way her left eye did. Something was wrong. She just wouldn't tell us what. Snow and Dully suspected it was her ex's fist. The loser had left town before the ink was dry on the divorce papers, thankfully. It looks to me like she didn't get out of that marriage unharmed, though.

She picked up the bouquet and thrust it at me. "This bouquet alone will have December eating out of your hand."

I took the flowers and stared down at them. Red miniature roses were surrounded by baby's breath. It was beautiful, and something you would expect to see a bride holding on her wedding day. The paper was blue and covered in snowflakes, and the ribbon added the final touch.

"These are beautiful, Savan." I laid them back on the counter and reached for my wallet in the side pocket of Sport.

"Beautiful flowers for a beautiful woman. Now, you better hurry so you aren't late," she said, coming around the counter.

I opened my wallet, but she laid her hand over mine and shook her head. "You deserve a wonderful gal like December. No payment needed, just make sure I get an invitation to the wedding." She leaned down to kiss my cheek and I hugged her tightly.

"Thanks, Savannah. It's just a thank you dinner, but I promise if there is a wedding, you'll be the first to know."

She held the door for me while I wheeled through and I turned then, gazing up at her. "Savannah, promise me you'll have that eye looked at. We're worried about you."

Her left eye darted around the town square, avoiding mine. "Okay, I promise."

But the promise was hollow.

Chapter Four

December

"You look fabulous, dahling," Garrett said from the kitchen.

I did a curtsy and fluffed my hair a little bit. "Thank you kindly, sir."

He shook his head at me and grinned. "You're doing an awful lot of dressing up for *just dinner*, December." He flipped his hands around in the air with the knife he was using to chop potatoes.

I stuck my nose up in the air and turned back to the mirror. "Well, you never take me out," I huffed and he snorted, throwing the knife in the sink. He strode towards me and pulled me into his arms before he dipped me.

I burst into giggles that made my leg sticking up in the air shake comically. Soon he was giggling just as hard and had to set me up on my feet before we both fell down.

"I'd love to take you out, lovie, it's just not in the cards for us." He gave a heavy sigh and slunk back to the kitchen, dropping the potatoes into the stew.

"I suppose Sage wouldn't like it much if she

found out you were dating other women." I grinned and he flinched.

"You've met her, right? She trusts you, and only you. That's the only reason you're living here. I'm gonna miss you when you're gone," he sang.

I flinched and unfortunately, he noticed. He came back over and rubbed my upper arms. "We aren't going to kick you out. We will always have a spare room here for you."

I sighed at his words. "I can't stay once Sage gets back from her mom's. I know I need to find a place, and I've run out of time."

He shook his head. "Just because Sage will be back in a week doesn't mean you've run out of time. We love you, and you can stay as long as you want to."

"I'm looking for a place, I really am. A small efficiency isn't easy to find right now and to be honest, I don't want to live with just anyone. I'm getting kind of old for roommates." I winked and he laughed.

"You're ancient, it's true, but I understand. I can put some feelers out at work if that would help." He ran for the kitchen and grabbed the stew pot before it boiled over.

I stood and checked my hair in the mirror, making sure it hadn't fallen from the french braid I'd put it in earlier. All was intact and I nodded at myself in the mirror. "At this point, anything would help. Do these pants make me look fat?" I asked, doing a three-sixty spin for him to check.

"Oh, this is serious. I got the *is my butt fat* question." He waved his fingers at me and I tossed my hand on my hip.

"I didn't ask if my butt was fat, but thanks for pointing that out. Now I know it is," I groaned.

His hands were waving in the air now. "Sorry, flashback to college days when you asked me that every day. I cross my heart and swear on my mother's grave that your butt isn't fat."

I huffed and crossed my arms over my chest. "I work with your mother, Garrett. She's not dead."

He just grinned at me, and I checked the clock. I still had ten minutes before Jay would be here to pick me up. I debated changing my pants, but steeled my shoulders and smoothed my blouse down. I'm done trying to be someone I'm not. That song with the lyrics *take me as I am* ran through my mind and I rolled my eyes towards the ceiling. I've never had great self-esteem, but at twenty-five, maybe it was time to stop pretending to be anyone but who I am.

"So, do I need to grill this guy?" Garrett asked from the kitchen where he hummed while he started chopping carrots.

"No, he's the brother of a friend I work with, and from a very well respected family. I'm not worried, besides this isn't a date. This is just dinner. He's thanking me for giving him a ride when his tire got a nail in it," I informed him.

He groaned. "You aren't picking up guys off the side of the road again, are you?"

I gave him the so-so hand. "He wasn't on the side of the road. He was on the sidewalk."

I turned and grabbed my scarf, tucked it around my neck, and then shrugged into my coat.

"Did he go off the road? Sounds serious, December, was he okay?"

"He got a flat on his wheelchair, Garrett. He needed a ride back to his truck to get a spare tube."

He shook his finger at me. "Don't even mess with me here, Ember. That's not funny."

I rolled my eyes heavenward and they landed back on him. "I'm not messing with you, Rhett," I emphasized and he pursed his lips. "He's in a wheelchair and he ran over a nail. What's the big deal?"

He held his hands up. "Nothing, it's not a big deal. I just thought you were kidding. Sorry, won't happen again."

I buttoned my coat and nodded. "His truck was at the hospital. It turns out he interviewed for the social worker position that's open. Since I was going there, I gave him a lift."

"Is he picking you up here, or are you driving?" he asked, pointing to the door.

"He's picking me up, why?"

He did a facepalm. "There are four stairs that lead to the front door. Maybe you should go wait outside?"

It was my turn to purse my lips. "Excellent point. That's why you're the smart one." I grinned, gave him a peck on the cheek, and grabbed my pocketbook. "Ta-ta for now. Don't wait up."

When I closed the door behind me, I could hear him laughing.

Jay

I glanced at the bouquet on the passenger seat and took a deep breath. *It's just dinner with a new friend, Jay, nothing more.* I nodded my head to the mantra that played through my mind. The voice on the GPS directed me to an older neighborhood where the houses were small with neatly manicured lawns and well-built porches. Well-built porches that all harbored four or five stairs to get to the front door. I swallowed hard. I wasn't going to get up the stairs to pick her up properly. I'd have to call her from the sidewalk. Wow, what a great way to start off a date. I laughed and the sound was loud inside the truck. "It's not a date, Jay. Besides, getting a flat on your wheelchair and requiring a tow back to your truck probably was a good indication of your weakness, you idiot," I scolded myself, shaking my head. "Forget about it, man. She knows you sit in a chair. She could have said no, but she said she wanted to get to know you better. Just let it go and play it out."

I had to quit talking to myself, at least out loud, I decided and clamped my lips shut for the rest of the trip.

"Turn left on Larson's Commons in ten feet." The GPS voice said and I used the hand control to brake and signal my left turn. I crawled down the street, taking my hands off the wheel long enough to punch the annoying GPS woman's voice to mute. December told me her address was 1413 Larson's Common. The numbers were getting bigger with each house and then I saw her.

She was standing on the porch, her long brown coat stopping midcalf as she leaned against the railing. She was waiting for me and I couldn't help but smile. I was worried about nothing because she already had my back again. The truck came to a rolling stop in front of her house and she waved from the porch, taking the stairs slowly without taking her eyes from mine. I rolled the window down and leaned over the bench seat.

"Let me come around and help you in," I said quickly, unbuckling my seatbelt, but she held up her hand.

"I can open the door myself."

"It's what a gentleman does," I insisted.

"I'll make you a deal, let me get in this time and you can help me out at the restaurant. There isn't a break in the sidewalk anywhere," she stated matter of fact and I caught her drift.

"Deal." I smiled, lifting the bouquet from the seat when she pulled the door open. She slipped one boot covered calf inside my truck and I stifled a moan. When she slid the rest of herself onto the leather seat, I couldn't help but notice how well her backside filled out her pants, and then I really had to get a grip on my breathing.

"These are for you. Thank you for saving the day. I really appreciate your willingness to pick up a total stranger off the street and give him a ride," I joked.

She blushed and accepted the roses. "These are gorgeous," she said while inhaling the scent.

"Not as gorgeous as you are," I admitted and then hit myself in the forehead. "Sorry, that just slipped out."

"Thank you for the flowers, and the compliment, Jay. I don't know any woman who would want you to apologize for calling her gorgeous," she said shyly, staring at the flowers.

I smiled widely and pointed at the house. "I suppose you should go put those in some water before we leave. I didn't even think of that until now."

She felt the bottom of the paper Savannah had wrapped them in. "Whoever made the bouquet put floral water tubes on every stem. They will be fine for a few hours while we eat."

Of course, she did, I thought to myself. I pulled back onto the street and nodded toward the flowers, my hands busy with the controls. "Snow's best friend, Savannah, put those together. Have you met Savannah Hart?"

"Yes! I love her shop. She has so much unique and eccentric décor. I stop in and bring her a coffee some weekends. She always looks so worn out running the place by herself."

I peeked at her from the corner of my eye and then back to the road, my lips barely curving.

"What?" she asked innocently.

"I told Savannah who I was picking up tonight and she was all *I know her, she works out at the hospital gym with Snow.*"

She grinned at my imitation of Savannah's voice. "I do work out at that gym, actually. Maybe she just didn't want you to be intimidated by the fact that I'm lonely and hang out at her shop on the weekend." She laughed airily and the sound was a little like a flute floating on the wind.

"Knowing Savannah, that's exactly what she was doing. Not the lonely part, just the part about not wanting me to know she knows you. She also said you're gorgeous. So, you're lonely?" I asked, sounding like a fool. "I'm sorry. I'm really nervous."

She laid her hand on my shoulder. "Don't apologize. I'm nervous, too. Sometimes I'm lonely. I don't know a lot of people here yet and Savannah is so, so …" she waved her hand around.

"Fantastically funny, freakishly knowledgeable, and a fun friend?" I finished and she gave me a nod.

"To a T. She seems a little lonely lately, too. I've been stopping in to see her more often. I'm worried about her eye. I guess it's the nurse in me."

I glanced at her quickly then forced my eyes back to the road. "I'm not a nurse and I'm worried, too. Snow is downright fit to be tied."

"Really?" she asked and I nodded. "I think Snow and I better have an intervention with her."

"Oh boy, now I feel kind of sorry for Savannah," I teased and she did that laugh again that made my chest feel less tight.

"Where are we going for dinner?" she asked as I made a left turn into a parking lot.

"Here."

She glanced up at the sign. "The Firebush? I've never been here, but I've heard the food is outstanding."

I parked the truck and turned it off. "They have excellent food, the best being the chicken marsala followed closely by the beef tips."

I turned and she was exiting the truck already. She was around to the driver's side in the blink of an eye.

"Hey, we made a deal!"

"Oh, I forgot! I'm nervous," she said again and I could see by the look in her eyes she wasn't kidding.

I took her hand off the car door and brought it to my lips, kissing it gently. "Don't be nervous, I don't bite. Let me get Sport so we can celebrate."

She looked in the back of the truck and raised an eyebrow. "Sport? What the heck? You got a new chair since I saw you last?"

She reached in and lifted it from the back of the truck and I held my finger up with my mouth open, but the chair was already resting on the tires.

"I have a lift for that, you know. I don't want

you to hurt yourself." I reached down and pushed the red button and Sport unfolded himself while December's eyes went wide.

"It doesn't weigh anything, and damn that's cool. This resembles Snow's chair, did you get a MAC, too?" she asked, walking around the back of the chair and squatting down. Her coat pulled back and her strong thighs flexed under her pants. I glanced away to keep from embarrassing myself on the first date. Great, now it's a date. I shook my head and pulled the chair next to me, so I could slide in.

"It's a new prototype, Snow and Dr. James developed. I guess they've been working on it for years. She brought it home yesterday and asked me to test drive it. I really hope they don't make me give it back. I've only had it for a few hours and I'm already in love," I admitted.

"If this chair can do what Snow's does, I can see why. Wait. What are we celebrating? The chair?" she asked, replaying my words in her mind.

I shook my head. "Nope, we're celebrating my new position as a social worker at Providence Hospital."

"Oh, my gosh, Jay! That's so wonderful, congratulations," she whispered, throwing her arms around my shoulders and hugging me to her.

She smelled of sweet musk and fresh soap that left me almost breathless. Her warm arms around my shoulders were soothing and I tentatively hugged her back.

"Thank you, I'm extremely happy. It's the job I needed to stay close to home. I don't think I can stand to be away from Sunny."

She pulled back from the hug and I reluctantly let her go. "Sunny is such a sweetheart. I can see why you can't be without her. She has an uncanny ability to comfort without even knowing she's doing it. She's really special."

I nodded, taking her hand. "She was the balm to my soul I didn't know I needed until they laid her in my arms. Okay, enough sappy, let's go celebrate." I grinned, hitting the small switch to activate voice recognition. "Sport, forward, hands."

The chair started rolling and she walked next to me, our hands entwined. She shook her head a little bit at the chair. "Just so cool," she whispered.

Chapter Five

We were moving hand in hand down the paved walkway to the lake, which was the focal point of Snowberry, Minnesota. Snowberry Lake was a favorite destination for every family in town. In the summer, the leaves surround the lake-walk, making it a cool and comfortable place to sit and watch the kids splashing in the water, and the families picnicking on the grass. In the fall, the leaves are vibrant colors and the mountain ash trees are heavy with berries. In the winter, the berries that didn't fall are covered in a white coat of snow, hence the name, Snowberry Lake.

"Dinner was wonderful, thank you, Jay." December squeezed my hand and I looked up into her chocolate brown eyes.

"I'm supposed to be thanking you, remember. I'm happy you enjoyed it. The chicken marsala?"

"Amazing." She grinned and I squeezed her hand.

"It's starting to look like winter is upon us," I lamented and she stopped, pulling my hand towards a bench that overlooked the still water.

She sat down, still not releasing my hand, but

I slowly pulled it out and locked Sport then hauled myself onto the bench next to her. She smiled when I laid my arm on the back of the bench.

"Winter is my favorite season. It must be the name." She giggled and I let my hand drop to her shoulder where my thumb rubbed it absently. I pretended the goosebumps I saw appear on her neck were from the wind.

"December is a great name. Should I guess your birthday?" I joked and she snorted.

"Well, you have thirty-one tries to get it right."

"Okay, let's see, December first?" I asked and she turned and stared at me.

"Wow, you're good." She laughed and shook her head.

"It just made sense."

"I was born at exactly midnight on December first. My twin brother, Noel, was born a few minutes later." She shared the information like it was a grocery list and I couldn't hide the surprise on my face.

"You have a twin? That's so cool. I always wanted to be a twin. Does he live nearby?"

She shook her head in a funny half-shake and half-shrug. "He lives in Rochester, at least the last I knew. We don't talk much."

She pulled her coat around her tighter, and it wasn't from the cold. Her body language told me talking about her brother wasn't something she liked doing.

"I'm sorry. I have three brothers and a sister,

so I know they can be pretty annoying, but we get along well, all in all." I trailed off and stared out over the lake. "I sure am glad I get to stay in Snowberry. Do you like it here?" I asked, trying to turn the conversation away from family.

"I love it here. I've experienced all the town has to offer for every season, and I like it better than Rochester," she answered, laying her hand on my knee.

"Really? Rochester is a big city compared to Snowberry." I subtly laid my hand over hers, but she didn't pull away.

"Rochester is always busy and there's never any downtime. Here, when I'm not at the hospital, I enjoy how quiet the town is. I always tell Garrett I like that they roll up the sidewalks at nine because it gives you the feeling of old-world charm. That said, the town is still extremely tech-savvy and the medical care is still second to none. Kind of the best of both worlds, one could say."

I lifted my hand off hers and rested my other one back on the bench, moving away from her a little. "Garrett? I didn't know anything about a boyfriend." I grimaced and she turned to me, her eyes big.

"No, Garrett is just a friend. Well, not just a friend. He's my best friend, but not like a best best friend." She groaned, tucking a hair under the hat on her head. "He's my roommate, has been since college. I live with him, and his wife, Sage, at the house you picked me up at. I'm looking for a place of my own."

"I see, well, then do you mind if I hold your hand again?" I asked, smirking a little and she laid her hand over mine.

"I don't mind at all, but enough about me, Jay Alexander. You kept me busy talking about myself all the way through dinner, now it's time for you to tell me just who Jay is. Inquiring minds want to know."

I thought I had managed to keep the focus on her for the night. "Not much to tell, really. I'm just a Minnesota boy who likes watching the Vikings get their butts kicked every Sunday, and wants to make his family proud."

She turned to me and smiled. "I know for a fact you make Snow proud. She's always telling me a story about you at work. It makes me feel like I know you already, so I know there is more to you than watching the Vikings."

I shook my head with exasperation. "She has got to learn how to let a man be mysterious."

"I don't like mysterious. I don't like games. I don't like putting on airs and I don't like pretending I'm somebody I'm not."

I raised both brows as high as they would go. "I was kidding, December. I don't like those things, either. Though, sometimes I pretend I'm somebody I'm not. It happens when you're a model."

"A model?" she asked, shocked.

I closed her mouth with my finger before I spoke. "What? A guy in a wheelchair can't be a model?" I joked and the look in her eye said she knew she hurt me. "That was a joke, sweetheart." I rubbed her shoulder until some of the tension disappeared.

"What kind of model are you?" she finally asked.

"Not a pants model, that's for sure," I teased and she finally laughed and swatted at my coat. "I was a model for all kinds of things, but mostly suits and dress clothes. The best part was getting to keep whatever I wore, which has helped build my wardrobe significantly."

She ran a hand under my lapel. "I noticed you like a fine suit, so do I, by the way. You sure can pull off the GQ look. I just had no idea you that you model."

I held up a finger. "Modeled. My final contract expired and I'm getting out of the business. It was a great way to put myself through college, but it's time for a real job. Modeling required me to work out constantly to keep my upper body buff. It was starting to take a toll on my back." I surprised myself admitting that, and snapped my jaw shut. I never talk about my back with anyone, much less someone I just met. "Now, at least I can work out the way I want to."

"Is that why you're in the chair? Did you have an accident?" she asked and I stared at her blank-faced.

"You don't know?" I gazed into her eyes, look-ing for any sign that she knew the real reason, but there was none. "Snow hasn't told you?"

She shook her head. "She seemed to have left that part out. I didn't even know you were in a chair until we met the other day. I guess she doesn't see that about you."

I moved my arm back around and debated swinging into my chair and calling it a night.

"You don't have to tell me, Jay. I understand." She stood and walked to the edge of the sidewalk to look out at the stars over the lake. "The stars are especially bright tonight, even with the moon almost full."

I stayed on the bench and took a cleansing breath of the night air. "With age, I've struggled to tell people about my condition. When I was a kid, I never had a problem with it. I was just Jay Alexander, the boy next door in the wheelchair. Then I got to college and all of that changed. I've learned kids are accepting without explanations, but adults sometimes forget that lesson when they hit their teenage years."

She kept her back to me but nodded. "You're absolutely right, Jay. We teach our kids to have empathy and not to judge people, but then we turn around and do it to others. Like I said, I understand. Besides, being Jay Alexander isn't about being in a chair. I've already learned that in the few hours we've spent together tonight."

I laughed softly and thought back to dinner when we had shared wine, talked about sports, and tried each other's dinners. I listened intently

KATIE METTNER

as she told me about college and following Garrett to Snowberry when Providence Hospital came calling. She has a true love for nursing people back to health, and I felt a connection to her I had never felt with a woman before. A connection between two people who like to help others so they could forget about their own problems for a little while.

"I was born with spina bifida. My mom didn't know she was pregnant with me until she was almost five months along. She thought she was done having babies and never considered the thought that she might be pregnant. I was born with a lesion at about L5."

"So you're the baby of the family?" she asked, turning and walking back to the bench.

I'm sure my mouth was hanging open when she sat next to me. "Yeah, I'm the baby of the family. My brother, Bram, is next, Dully, Jake, and then my sister, Mandy, is the oldest. Dully became a special education teacher because he wanted to help other kids like me. We tend to be overlooked as contributors to the classroom, even if all we have is a physical disability. Dully has taught me a lot."

She laid her hand on my knee again and gazed up at me. "Is that why you guys are so close?"

"We were inseparable growing up, even though he's a lot older than I am. We just have the same kind of soul, I guess. He never let me miss out on anything I wanted to do as a kid, even if he had to carry me. We played hockey, went roller skating, and played football and baseball. He took me to the

52

lake to swim and held me the whole time. I can't move my legs, so swimming is a challenge, but when I was with him, it was like I was free from everything."

"He sounds like a great big brother." She smiled, and I did, too.

"He was, is, even with his own family to take care of now."

"Is that why your back hurts? The spina bifida?"

I did the so-so hand. "That specific spot can be irritable, but this new chair is helping. I think I just pulled something in my midback and it's taking time to heal. I'm sure it will be fine once I'm not stressed about finding a job. I'll do more stretching and less weightlifting and it will come around."

"I did a stint in rehab at Mayo for one of my rotations. I learned some great massage techniques there. I'd gladly give you one if you want, strictly professional, of course," she added quickly.

"I'm going to save that information in my back pocket for a rainy day, December. As long as you don't mind, I can't promise it would be strictly professional for me," I added, not sure why I was flirting with this beautiful woman who had no reason to be here with me tonight. I could tell she didn't know what to say, so I motioned to the sidewalk. "Well, I suppose I should be getting you home."

She glanced up and shrugged a little. "I'd love to stay here a while longer with you if that's okay."

I put my right arm around her and she leaned

against my shoulder. Sitting next to a beautiful woman on a park bench under the stars was something I was completely okay with.

KISS

December

"Jay, the house is up there." I pointed and he nodded, putting the key in his pocket and opening his door. He punched some buttons on a remote and the lift hoisted Sport out of the truck and onto the ground.

"I know, but I want to walk you to your door." He winked and slid into the chair, closing the door. I watched in the mirror as he rolled behind the truck and up the sidewalk ramp. Next thing I knew he was opening my door and reaching for my hand. I picked the flowers up off the seat and cradled them in my arm, the sight of them still causing butterflies in my tummy. I took his hand and stood on the boulevard, so he could close the door.

"Sport, forward, hands," he said, and we walked up the sidewalk toward Garrett's house.

"I love how this town is always so quiet. It's enjoyable to be able to walk down the sidewalks and not be afraid," I mused, and he squeezed my hand in response.

"Snowberry is pretty safe, but a single woman walking around after dark needs to be careful," he warned and I chuckled.

"Don't worry, the city mouse in me would never let the country mouse forget about the dangers," I assured him, slowing my steps as we approached the house. Garrett had left the porch light on and we walked up the walkway and stopped at the bottom of the steps. I turned and sat on the second step up, level with where he sat in the chair.

"Thank you for saving my butt the other day, and for celebrating the new job with me tonight. I had a very nice time," he said quietly.

I took his hand and held it in mine. "You're welcome, I'm glad I got to be your knightette in shining armor. Tonight was wonderful." I held up the flowers. "These are beautiful."

"So are you."

"Do you start the new job this week?" I asked, changing the subject.

"I have a few orientation things to attend, but I won't start the job for a few weeks. It will give me a little bit more time to get Sunny used to going back to preschool and spending less time in her day with me."

"Poor little thing, she's going to have to readjust, but at least she will still see you on the weekends."

"I just live a few hundred yards from their house. She has a well-worn path to my door. I think we will get used to it quickly. She starts school next year, and it's important she goes this year for some early socialization. She spends most of her time with adults and I think sometimes she forgets how to be a kid."

"You speak of her like she's your own daughter. She's a lucky little girl."

"Nah, she's the reason I'm sitting here today. The day she was born, I realized the universe is much bigger than me, and I better get my head on straight or I was going to miss out on a lot." His voice was firm, but there was an edge to it. That made me wonder just what he needed to get straight.

"I have to work early, so I should be going in. Maybe I can make you dinner Thursday night? I don't have to work," I said quickly, letting the words out before I talked myself out of it.

His eyes went wide and he smiled. "You want to make me dinner?"

"Yes, that's where I cook food and then put it on a plate for you to eat. Are you familiar with that?" I asked cheekily, and he chuckled.

"I've done it a few times. I'd love for you to make me dinner, but, uh…" He motioned at the stairs. "Is there a back door?"

I grimaced and shook my head. "Not one without stairs. Shoot, I'm sorry. I didn't even think about that."

"You're welcome to cook dinner at my place. I have full kitchen amenities and a fireplace."

I clapped my hands excitedly. "It's a deal. I'll get directions from Snow and be there at say, four?"

I could tell he was surprised, but he nodded.

"Text me and let me know what we're having. I'll get the wine," he whispered, his voice husky and his deep blue eyes shuttered.

"I will. I'm looking forward to it. I want to get to know you better, Jay, if that's okay," I stammered, and he lifted my hand to his lips and kissed it.

"I'm looking forward to it, too. Do you think your roommate is watching? I'd really like to kiss you goodnight," he explained, his eyes trained on the door over my shoulder.

"He's not even home," I whispered.

He leaned forward, and I met him halfway, our lips touching tentatively, my eyes fluttering closed. His strong hands held my shoulders and his lips massaged mine until I whimpered under my breath when he pulled away.

"Thank you for the wonderful company, December. I'll stay here until you're safely inside, and I'll see you again on Thursday?" he asked, rubbing my arms and I nodded.

"It's a date," I said, standing up and climbing the last two steps to the porch. I shifted the flowers in my arm and slipped the key inside the lock, pushing the door open.

I stepped over the stoop and then turned and waved at him. He raised his hand and waved back before I closed the door. I inhaled the sweet scent of the roses and smiled a dreamy smile. "It's a date," I said to the empty room. "It's a date."

Chapter Six

Jay

"I didn't figure I'd see the whites of your eyes until much later today," Dully said, handing me a barbell.

I took it and started doing slow curls with my right arm. "We weren't out late since she had to work today. I know you're wondering, so yeah, we had a good time. She's fantastic to talk to and beautiful to boot. I haven't enjoyed myself that much since Sunny made me brownies in her Easybake oven."

He snorted and almost dropped his barbell. "Well, that's some high praise for this woman. Are you going to see her again?"

"Yeah," I said, my voice strained as I tried to lift the weight with my left hand. "She's coming over to make me dinner Thursday night." I dropped the barbells to the floor and wiped the sweat off my face. "That's it. I'm done."

"Come on, man. You can do one more set," Dully insisted, but I shook my head and bent to the left, trying to get the kink out of my back.

"No, I really can't. Something is up with my

back," I admitted. The sharp, shooting pain that zinged along my spine reminded me of who was boss.

I saw the concern in Dully's eyes as I straddled the bench in the garage. Our free weights sat next to the old workbench he'd taken from dad's garage. We'd been working out together since I moved back home in June, but I'd been slowing down lately. Even he'd noticed. "Is that still bothering you?"

I nodded, reaching around with my right arm to rub the tender spot near my ribcage. "Yeah, I'm afraid it is. I think I might have to cave and go into the clinic."

"You do that and Snow will think she's won." Dully smiled, picking up the weights and setting them back on the rack.

I slung my towel around my neck. "Well, she will have. Your wife is a real tough cookie. I'm actually glad she's not a practicing doctor. She scares me."

Dully bent over at the waist, his shoulders shaking at the thought of his brother being afraid of his tiny, wheelchair-bound wife, but I was. I loved Snow like a sister, but man, she's smart, and you can't pull a thing over on her. My slight miscalculation the other day in asking her advice had earned me nothing but hard stares and heavy sighing for two days.

"Jason, she loves you, that's why she doesn't want you to let an injury go," he said, straightening up and grabbing his own towel.

I tossed my hand at him and let it fall when the movement caused pain. "I know, but with the new job starting, I think we better take the next couple of days off from the weights. Maybe I'm just overdoing it."

"If you willingly agree to days off from weights, then you are going to be seen tomorrow. If you don't, I'll have Snow call Mom." Dully smiled triumphantly as he played his trump card, crossing his arms over his chest.

I shook my finger at him. "Oh, no, that's playing dirty. That's worse than playing dirty," I sputtered.

"You said it yourself, you have a new job to start and you can't do that when you're hurting," Dully insisted.

I held up my hands. "Let me soak in the tub and see if it improves. If it's not better, I'll go after my orientation on Tuesday," I promised.

I swung my leg over the bench and transferred into Sport. The movement of my body made the cramp in my back lock down and I bent over at the waist, barely able to breathe.

Dully was next to my chair instantly, staring up at me from below. I opened my eyes long enough to see the petrified look on his face. "Let's go to the hospital," I said through gritted teeth, and he picked up his phone.

"No ambulance." I huffed.

"I'm calling Snow. I need her van," Dully said,

hitting a button.

It hurt to breathe, and my ribcage was tight and on fire. Suddenly, I was gasping for air. I couldn't draw any into my lungs, and I reached out to grab Dully's leg. He grabbed me as the room grew dark and the pain finally faded.

KISS

I woke up slowly, disoriented and confused. I came to briefly in the ER once they gave me oxygen, but I couldn't move my left arm and I freaked out. After that, everything was kind of a blur from the medications they had given me.

I tried to lift my left arm up off the stretcher and was rewarded with my fingers waving in front of my face. I let out a heavy breath and lifted the oxygen mask off my face. I glanced around, turning my head left and then right, trying to figure out where I was.

A hand came down on my shoulder as the blood pressure cuff began to inflate on my right arm. "You're in recovery. Surgery is over and it went very well," a sweet voice said. She lifted the oxygen mask off my head and slipped the oxygen tube in my nose instead. "You need to leave that on right now, okay, Jason?"

The nurse finally moved into my line of sight and I groaned. Now I was hallucinating. I was hallucinating that December was my nurse. I guess it's true what they say, your psyche does weird things under the influence of drugs.

"Just call me Jay. I hate Jason," I muttered while I rubbed my eyes.

She turned to me and laughed, the same sound from last night, and I shook my head a little. "Dully told me to use your real name and you'd wake up right quick. Looks like he was right."

I squinted at her name badge, but couldn't read it. "December?" I asked, my voice hoarse, but shocked.

She stopped and picked up my right hand, squeezing it for a second. "Hi, yeah, it's me. I was just coming out of the locker room when Dully flagged me down. You don't remember?"

I shook my head. "Not really. I remember getting to the ER and then not being able to feel my arm. What the hell happened?"

"They found a ruptured disc at T6. Pieces of the disc were compressing the nerves in your diaphragm, essentially paralyzing it. That's why you suddenly couldn't breathe. Lifting weights today probably pushed you over the edge," she chastised.

I groaned. "Snow is never going to let me live this down." I threw my arm over my face, only to be rewarded with the I.V. tube hitting me in the eye.

December chuckled and checked the machines. "I have a feeling she's probably going to say *I told you so,* but she loves you and worries about you. Your whole family is in the waiting room. Is it okay if I call and tell them you're awake?"

I nodded and she picked up a phone on a portable computer cart. She spoke for a minute, and then her laughter floated through the air. I closed my eyes and tried to sort through what she said.

"December?" I called and she came over, checking my pulse. "Why did they do surgery?"

"They had to take out the disc. It was causing some major problems for your arm and chest. It certainly couldn't stay there." She patted my shoulder to keep me calm, but it wasn't working.

I moved my body a little, expecting a shock of pain, but none came. "I don't have any pain?"

"Is that a question or a statement?" she asked, chuckling a little.

"Why don't I have any pain? I'm not … paralyzed, am I?" I asked frantically and she laid her hand on my chest.

"No, you're just confused, sweetheart. Take a deep breath. Can you feel my hand?" she asked and I nodded. I could feel it and I laid my own hand over hers, I.V. and all.

"I'm sorry, my mind is cloudy," I admitted.

She leaned against the stretcher like she didn't have a care in the world. "Don't apologize. Cloudiness is to be expected. Dr. Brooks performed the surgery using a laser. He was able to take out the piece of the disc that was causing the problem and repair your back, all through an incision an inch long. In a few days, you'll feel good as new," she promised, but I stared at her dubiously.

"What about my legs?" I asked.

She looked down at my blanket-covered legs and back to me. "What about them?"

I clamped my lips shut and shook my head. "Never mind. I'm not making any sense."

She smiled again and rubbed my leg through the blanket. "I understand you have a lot of questions and once we move you upstairs, Dr. Brooks will come in and talk to you. Just relax and rest, it will help clear the fogginess."

"I have to stay here?" I asked frantically.

"Just for the night, Jay. It's already after eight." She went back to the portable computer cart, and I closed my eyes.

I focused on breathing in and out evenly, so my heart rate stayed even, but my mind was racing with the thought that suddenly, the one thing I had going for me was gone.

KISS

It was dark when I opened my eyes again. The room was filled with shadows, the door cracked just enough to let a stream of light in. I could hear activity at the nurse's station and the dinging of the elevator, but my room was quiet otherwise. Snow made sure I got the royal treatment and insisted on a private room, but it was lonely now that everyone was gone.

She and Dully finally left a few hours ago when I assured them I was fine. Snow didn't want to leave, but she was so completely exhausted that I was afraid soon she'd be the one in pain. Dully was a wreck because he felt guilty for letting me work out when I was obviously injured. I had to remind them that Sunny needed them to comfort her more than I needed them to sit and stare at me, and they were gone.

I heard the soft whisper of clothes rubbing together and glanced around the room. I was certain I was alone or had a nurse snuck in to check the monitors again? I raised the head of my bed and noticed a figure on the small loveseat by the window. My eyes brought her into focused and I saw the dark brown hair falling over the beautiful, relaxed face of December Kiss. She was still in her scrubs, which told me she came straight here after her shift ended. From where I was, I could see her bottom as she rested on her side. Her feet were scrunched up and her knees were bent, hanging over the edge of the loveseat.

"December?" I whispered.

She jumped up, her eyes wild and her hands going to her neck for her stethoscope. Her hands grabbed air and she patted her chest.

"December, you're okay. I wasn't sure if it was you. What are you doing here?"

She padded to my bed and checked my I.V. and fixed my blankets. "I promised Snow I'd stay when my shift was over."

I slipped my hand in hers and squeezed it a little. "Thank you, but I'm okay. The night nurses will take care of me. You better go get some rest, you have to work tomorrow."

"I've been sleeping for a couple of hours already. You're a very easy patient." She winked and I chuckled a little.

"You don't look very comfortable with your legs all scrunched up like that. I'm sure your bed would feel a lot better," I encouraged, but she shook her head.

"I'm not going home, Jay. Now, do you need some more pain meds? Your I.V. is almost empty, so I'm going to grab a new bag." She motioned to the door now that her nurse mode had engaged.

I grabbed her hand and wouldn't let it go. "I know you're off the clock right now. Let the other nurses worry about the bag and the pain meds. You need to rest."

She finally nodded and stretched, staring at the loveseat like it was a force to be reckoned with. My head was much clearer now that the drugs had worn off and I kept hold of her hand. She finally turned back to me.

"Wanna share my bed?" I asked and her eyes grew to the size of saucers.

"Nah, I don't think I'll fit," she stuttered, taking a step back.

"I can be as stubborn as you are." I grinned and she gazed up at the ceiling and back to me.

I let go of her hand and moved carefully to the side of the bed, leaving more than enough room for her to settle on her side. I patted the spot and she stared at me for a moment and then sighed heavily. She stretched out on the bed on her side and I gave her a pillow to tuck behind her back. She rested against the rail of the bed and I lowered it flat.

"See, you fit just fine," I whispered and she didn't make eye contact.

"As long as I'm on my side," she said, holding her arm out over her hips and puffing out her cheeks.

I ran my finger down her face. "Please stop making fun of your body. Beauty is in the eye of the beholder and my eyes think you're beautiful." I trailed my hand down her arm and took her hand. She nodded once, which was all I was going to get. "I would lie on my side so you can lay flat," I started to say and she jumped straight up.

"No! Don't do that." She held my chest and I took her wrists with mine.

"I was going to say, but Dr. Brooks told me not to. Any other night I would, though." I smiled and she relaxed, climbing back onto the bed and resting her head on the edge of my pillow. "Did you work all day?"

She nodded, trying to hide a yawn. "I came on at six and was working a twelve. I had no idea you were here until Dully caught me coming out of the locker room. I agreed to be in recovery with you. I kept you there longer than need be, but I was worried about you. Snow was so tired by the time I got off shift, I started worrying about her. I promised to stay since my shift was over. It's okay, I don't have to work again until three tomorrow, so I have time to go home and shower in the morning."

I checked the clock and it read nearly two a.m. "Well, beautiful, it's already morning, so we better get some sleep."

Her eyes didn't meet mine and I stared her down. "Why do you always look away when I say you're beautiful?"

She just shrugged and closed her eyes. "Wake me up if you need anything, Jay."

Her words came out slow and tired. I rubbed her arm and in minutes, she was breathing evenly, her body relaxed.

"You are beautiful, December. So beautiful," I whispered, my eyes drifting closed.

Chapter Seven

"Uncle Jay! Uncle Jay! Give me a ride, Uncle Jay!" my niece called as she ran toward me.

I looked around frantically for something to protect myself with as she flew at me, but Dully stepped in and caught her in his arms. "Hey, my tiny snowflake, we talked about being careful around Uncle Jay for a few weeks, remember?"

Sunny took her daddy's face in her hands and frowned. "I forgetted daddy. I'm sorry."

"Come here, Sunshine, you can sit on my lap. Your daddy worries too much. Uncle Jay is just fine." I held my arms out and Dully frowned at me skeptically, but finally relented and set his daughter on my lap.

She kept her hands folded on her lap and looked up at me with big beautiful eyes. "Uncle Jay, I'm sorry your back hurts. When mommy's back hurts, I rub it. Do you want me to rub your back?"

I kissed her sweet-smelling cheek. "I'd love for you to rub my back. Should we go really slow into the living room and sit on the couch? I think I missed a couple episodes of Dora the Explorer. Wanna catch me up?"

She clapped her hands and nodded, trying to remember not to squirm. Dully stared at us disapprovingly, for about ten seconds, before he started laughing and shaking his head.

"Okay, go on, I'll bring the snacks," he promised, rummaging in the cupboard for some pretzels.

"Sport, forward, slow," I said to appease my brother. I was tired of everyone telling me to *be careful* and *go slow*. They'd been acting like I was ninety-five instead of twenty-five. Sunny was leaning back on my chest with her hands resting on my wrists, just like she had since she was old enough to sit up. She sits on her mommy's lap the same way.

"I love you, my sunny Sunshine," I sang, planting a kiss on her head.

She reached back and patted my cheeks. "I love you, my little Jaybird," she sang back. "I can't wait until we can go swimming again."

"Me either," I agreed, "but you know it's going to have to be inside now, right? It's too cold for the pond. Sport, stop," I said, and the chair halted next to the couch. She hopped off my lap and climbed up on the couch. "I think we can go out to the pool next week, as long as we're careful. Can we be careful?" I asked, winking, and she giggled, covering her mouth with her hands.

"We can be super careful. But we can't tell Daddy. He wouldn't be happy," she said sing-songy.

I tweaked her cheek and leaned back against

the soft couch.

"Uncle Jay, I can't rub your back if you're leaning on it, silly." Her little voice broke into my thoughts.

"How did you get so smart?" I asked, carefully pulling myself closer to the end of the couch, so she could rub my back.

"Where does it hurt?" she asked very grown-up, her fingers waving.

I pointed to the spot above my belt, a good safe distance away from the surgical site. Her fingers began to knead at the muscles in my back, and I leaned my elbows on my thighs and rested my chin in my hands.

"You know, Swiper would get what he was after if he waited until they couldn't see him before he swiped it," I mused.

She started to giggle. "But Uncle Jay, if he waited, then Dora couldn't tell us to yell 'Swiper no swiping!'. That's the whole point, silly!"

She may only be four, but she was already too smart for her own good. I'm relatively sure she gets that from her mom. Snow is a research doctor and has more degrees and accreditations than I can name.

"That feels good, Sun, but I need to sit back now, my legs are tired," I warned her and she scooted next to me so I could slide back. I slung my arm around her shoulder and took the bowl of pretzels from Dully when he came into the room. He plunked down in the chair and tossed his feet up on the hassock.

"How are you really feeling, Jay?" he asked me when Sun was enthralled in Dora.

"I'm feeling fine, really Dul, quit beating yourself up about this," I ordered him, and he shrugged.

"I shouldn't have let you keep lifting without getting that checked out. Things could have turned out much worse."

He'd been angry with himself for the last few days, and neither Snow nor I could get him to see he wasn't at fault. Sun climbed down off the couch and climbed up on his lap.

"Daddy, don't be sad," she said softly, rubbing the frown lines at his eyes. "It's not your fault that Uncle Jay hurt his back. He's stubborn, even Mommy says so."

I started to laugh, and Dully couldn't hide the smile that crept across his face. "He is stubborn, isn't he? But you know what? I like that about him, he never stops trying." Sunny put her arms around his neck and hugged him.

"She's right, I think Uncle Jay is very stubborn, but I love that about him," Snow said from the doorway.

I turned carefully and smiled at my sister-in-law. "Hi, Snow, I didn't hear you come in."

Dully let Sunny down off his lap and she ran to her mommy for a hug before she engrossed herself in Dora again.

"Hi, sweetheart, I wasn't expecting you home. Everything okay?" Dully asked.

"Everything is great. Mac forward," she ordered the chair and she stopped it at the couch. "I had a few hours free and came home to check on the patient. I know he was at the hospital earlier."

I rolled my eyes and shook my head. "Yes, Mommy, I had orientation today."

She leaned forward, her hand on her hip. "Jason Nicholas Alexander, you had surgery a few days ago. They didn't expect you at orientation today."

Dully snickered and I knew he wasn't going to help me with this one. I sighed heavily. "Snow, I can't afford to lose this job."

"Jay, they can't rescind their offer of employment because of this," she jumped in before I finished the sentence.

"I know, Snow, but I also don't want to give them any reason to regret the decision. I went in and filled out the paperwork they needed. They kept me quite comfortable the entire time. Besides, I'm not even in pain anymore."

"You may not be in pain, but you still have to be careful. You have to heal," she fretted and I held up my hands.

"Snow, I appreciate that you're always watching out for me, and I did ask them if I could break the next few orientations up into shorter days. They offered to give me four weeks off, but I respectfully declined. They need a social worker, and I need something to do. They agreed to let me work part-time over the next month and then start full-time when I feel I'm ready. I know in the past I haven't always made the best decisions, but I've grown up a lot. I know what I want from life and I know my limitations. I can compromise."

Her shoulders deflated and she leaned back against the chair. "You're right, I'm sorry. I've just been so worried about you."

I smiled when she climbed onto the couch for a hug. "I love you, Snow. You always make sure I'm safe, it means a lot to me."

My mom might worry about me less than this woman, but she meant well and I would in no way make her feel bad for being concerned about my well-being. "In fact, I forgot to thank you for asking December to stay with me Sunday night. She's pretty easy on the eyes when you wake up disoriented and out of sorts."

"December stayed with you Sunday night?" Snow asked, surprised.

I looked at her questioningly. "She said you didn't want to leave, and you made her promise to stay with me after her shift or you wouldn't go home."

She glanced at Dully and then back to me. "Oh, right. I was really tired." She cleared her throat and looked anywhere but at me. "I'm glad she was there for the night. I bet it helped to see a friendly face."

"You didn't ask her to stay with me for the night, did you?" I asked, reading her like a book.

"Can I plead the fifth on this?" She laughed, locking eyes with Dully.

I sat there smiling for a minute, thinking back to the vision of December asleep in my bed. She kept licking her lips every so often, her pink tongue darting out to wet her lips before she pulled it back inside that sweet mouth. Knowing she had come up there on her own made the memories even sweeter.

I cleared my throat. "Well, that's a new twist, moving on now," I joked, not wanting to make a big deal out of it. It was a big deal to me, but they didn't need to know that. "Listen, with this setback, I'm not going to be able to move out as soon as I thought. I have a security deposit saved, but Dr. Brooks said no heavy lifting for eight to twelve weeks. I know we said spring, but it might be summer at this point. I know you said it doesn't matter to you guys, but I just don't want you to think I'm not trying. I will pay rent once I get my first check, though. That's the least I can do."

Snow sat back against the couch and folded her arms. "Jay, we aren't kicking you out just because you got a job. You're welcome here for as long as you want to stay, you know that. We built the cottage for you and we don't want you to pay rent." She shrugged and I noticed some tears in her eyes.

"Snow, are you okay?" I asked, taking her hand.

She nodded and finally smiled. "I'm just so happy you got a job here in town. I don't think we'd know what to do without you here every day. We understand if you want to move into town or away from the family, but please know you don't have to."

"I don't want to move, Snow. I would miss you and Sunny too much. I spent a lot of years away at college and I hated it, but I can't continue to mooch off you and my brother. You have to let me start paying rent on the cottage once I have a steady pay-check," I insisted.

They built this house when she was first pregnant with Sunny, and it is fully handicapped accessible. Snow insisted they build a small two-bedroom cottage on the property as well, so I had a place to stay when I came home to visit. I could have stayed at my parents just across the pond, but I suppose, in her own way, she was giving me independence I would never get otherwise.

Dully got up and set Sunny on the chair, going to the desk in the corner of the room. He pulled an envelope out of the drawer and brought it over to Snow. "I think it's time we give him this," Dully said and she nodded. She turned and handed me the envelope.

"What's this?" I asked, surprised.

"Your real graduation present," Dully answered, running his hand through his hair.

"Guys, I graduated months ago, and you gave me a gift then," I reminded them.

Snow pointed at the letter. "That's actually your real graduation gift. We just didn't want to give it to you until you had a job."

"We didn't want it to influence where you looked for a position," Dully explained.

"I'm completely confused."

Dully motioned to the envelope and I opened it, reading the short letter inside, before glancing up to their excited and anxious faces. "You're giving me the cottage for graduation?"

"Like I said, we built that cottage for you." Snow smiled. "We want you to be part of Sunny's life and part of our life. All we ask is if you ever want to sell, we're allowed to buy the property back."

I shook my head and stared at the two people I loved so much. Dully and I had always been the closest of all the brothers. He'd taken care of me since I was a little boy, and he still was. Dully was my hero, and when he married Snow, she and I were instantly connected the same way.

"I don't know what to say," I admitted, reading the deed again. Not only had they given me the cottage, but an acre of land to go with it. "I really don't know what to say."

"Say you'll stay," Snow begged and I nodded.

"Oh, I'm staying. I just don't know how to thank you. The cottage? Are you sure?" I asked again and Dully laughed.

"We're one hundred percent sure. Your responsibilities will include your utilities and taxes, now that you have a job. If you need work done that you can't do, just let me know. The boys and I will do it, or we can hire it done. I love you, Jay. We're very proud of you. Congratulations on the job, I know it's the one you really wanted."

I nodded, my mind going a million miles a minute. "For one very important reason," I whispered, as she crawled up on my lap.

KISS

December

I pulled my Jeep to a stop at the entrance to a long blacktop driveway and checked the numbers again, A1478 Cherry Blossom Lane. Definitely the right place according to Snow's directions. I kept my foot planted firmly on the brake pedal and weighed my options. They were simple: turn around and go home or turn right down the driveway and make Jay dinner as promised. I didn't text him about the menu. Instead, I decided to pick up the wine myself. I was afraid he'd tell me not to come if he got the chance and I didn't want to give him a chance. Then again, maybe he really didn't want me to come. Maybe he wasn't feeling well and wanted to rest. So, why are you sitting here then?

I had a death grip on the steering wheel and ground my teeth together. I hadn't seen him since Monday when they released him, but Snow said he was feeling good and was up and around. The clock on the dashboard said three-fifty. *You better decide, woman.* I should trust my gut. I heaved out a sigh and turned right, following the turn in the blacktop driveway as it curved towards a beautiful log cabin nestled in a grove of trees. The leaves had fallen as winter approached and the trees were barren against the setting sun.

Snow told me to park by the garage and follow the short path through the woods to his cabin near the pond. I shut the engine off, and before I could lose my resolve, climbed from the Jeep and pulled the bag from the backseat. The handles cut into my hand and made me question myself again. I was setting the bag back in the Jeep when there was movement on the deck. Sunny was by the patio doors, waving shyly and I waved back.

Dully appeared behind her and gave me a thumbs-up sign. So much for escaping unnoticed. I brought the bag down to my side and held my head high, even though I wanted nothing more than to drop it into my hands. I headed down the path, one foot in front of the other, the butterflies in my stomach flitting around as the cottage grew near. The wind blew every so often, rustling the few leaves left on the branches. It was Mother Nature telling me in no uncertain terms that winter was on its way.

My steps faltered for a moment and I stopped when the full cottage came into view. It was straight out of a painting, with the long wooden logs perched perfectly on the next log, creating a rustic building block feel to the structure. A wooden deck ran the full length of the cabin, with multiple ramps and landings that opened into a full deck to overlook the pond. There was smoke drifting lazily from the fireplace, giving it a completely idyllic setting.

I walked up the ramps, noticing each time the wind blew, the smoke was blown every which way. A light shone inside and I thought I could hear music. I took a cleansing breath and set the bag on its bottom, wiping my hands on my ample thighs. *It's now or never, December.* I pushed the doorbell before I had a moment to rethink it. I waited nervously, bouncing from foot to foot.

"Doors open, Dully!" I heard a voice yell from inside and I bit my lip. I wasn't Dully and what if he was in a compromising position.

I pushed the door open and without looking inside the door, I answered him. "It's December, not Dully. Is it okay if I come in?"

The room was silent for almost a minute and I was just stepping back out onto the deck when the door opened the rest of the way. He sat in his chair and the expression on his face was shock.

"Good evening, December. To what do I owe the pleasure?" he asked, his arm motioning me in the door.

I picked up the bag and carried it across the threshold, standing there nervously with it in both hands. "I promised to cook you dinner tonight. It's almost four." I pointed at the clock, feeling a little silly to be explaining this. "I'm sorry. I shouldn't have come without calling."

He swung his chair around far enough to close the door and gazed up at me. "I didn't think you'd be coming tonight, but I'm glad you did."

The smile on my face relaxed a bit and I set the bag down on the floor. "Do you feel up to me staying? I understand if you don't."

He held his hand out. "Of course, let me take your coat. I'm not one to turn down a home-cooked meal."

I unbuttoned my coat and handed it to him, glancing around the room. "I feel like I'm standing in an idyllic storybook cottage. You must be sad to think about leaving this place."

When we talked at dinner the other night he told me he needed to find a new place, but it wasn't going to be easy, now I could see why. The cottage was set up with an open floor plan, which allowed him to move easily about the home in his chair, yet remained cozy and welcoming.

He turned Sport around and hung my coat on a wooden tree near the door, and when he turned back, he had an even bigger smile on his face. "I was sad about leaving and asked Dully and Snow if I could stay until spring. It turns out they never had any intention of me leaving."

He took my hand and led me to the couch, where I sat on the edge, nervously holding his hand. "What does that mean?"

He laughed happily. "They brought me the deed to the cottage and an acre of land today, telling me it was my real graduation present. They didn't want to give it to me before I found a job, in case I couldn't find one locally. When I landed the job at Providence, they knew I was here to stay. I'm not sure who was happier, them or me when they handed me that paper."

I patted his knee. "Sunny was probably the happiest of all."

He smiled that smile he always wore at the mention of her name. "She's been so sweet, coming to check on me every few hours. Snow gave her the newly found freedom of coming to my house by herself, since they can see the front door from the back deck, and she's using it liberally."

I opened my mouth to tell him I saw her when the doorbell rang again. He turned the chair and opened the door again to a little face.

"Hi, Uncle Jay, do you need anything?" Sunny asked, her little hands twisting in front of her.

"Yes, I need some sunshine, it's getting dark," he teased and she hugged him as best as she could with him in the chair.

"Mommy says I can't climb up on your lap with no one to help," she said, very grown-up, and I stood.

"I could help if you'd like," I added, and she peered up at me.

"I would like that very much, thank you," she said sweetly, and I lifted the little sprite up and settled her on Jay's lap.

He smiled up at me and mouthed, *thank you*. "Sunny, I'd like you to meet my friend December."

I knelt down by Jay's chair and ruffled her hair. "We've met, but it's nice to see you again, Sunny."

"It's nice to see you again, December. You have

a fun name like me and my mommy. December is the last month of the year. It's when Christmas is!" she said, wiggling on Jay's lap. He held her little hips still and kissed the top of her head.

"You're right on all accounts. It is great to have a fun name that no one else has, isn't it? Do you know what my last name is?" I asked and she shook her head. "Kiss. My name is December Kiss."

She held her hand to her mouth and blew a kiss, which I caught in midair. "That's the best name ever!"

"Thank you. Your Uncle Jay says you've been taking very good care of him the last few days."

She nodded her head vigorously. "He needs lots and lots and lots of TLC, Daddy says."

I smiled at Jay and winked at Sunny. "I'm a nurse and I agree. You can never have too much TLC after surgery."

She hugged him carefully around his neck and then scooted down until her feet touched the ground. "It was nice to see you, December. If you're a nurse, you can take care of my little Jaybird for me. Just remember, he likes his hot cocoa with lots of marshmallows."

Jay chuckled and tugged her little ponytail while I opened the door for her. "Thanks for stopping by, Sunny. I promise to take good care of him."

She skipped back up the path and I closed the door softly, bracing one foot up against it. "How do you stand that much cuteness all the time?"

"It's the reason I can't move away. I'd miss that

sunshine day after day." He smiled, picking up the bag and settling it on his lap, wheeling to the kitchen.

I followed him in and took the bag off his lap, setting it on the counter. "Let me do that, you're not supposed to be lifting stuff. Can I make you some hot chocolate?" I asked, my voice lilting like Sunny's did.

"Do you like hot chocolate?" he sparred back and I nodded, one hand on my hip.

"I love it, but not that icky packet stuff, it has to be made with real milk and real chocolate. Oh, and of course, lots of marshmallows."

"So, you're one of those gourmet chocolate lovers." He wheeled to the fridge and grabbed a bottle of milk. He held it out to me and raised a brow. "Put your money where your mouth is then, missy."

I took the bottle from him and grinned. "Better get ready to weep."

KISS

Jay

My hot chocolate was throwing steam into the air as I blew on the mixture of milk and marshmallows. December was in the kitchen at the sink and I was on the couch, resting my back.

When the clock crept closer to four and she hadn't called or texted, I assumed she wasn't coming. How very wrong I was. She came, with a full sack of food, a bottle of wine, and a beautiful smile.

I hid my face behind my mug and perused her body. This was the first time I'd been able to see her with no coat or uniform since our first dinner together. She was wearing a long sweater that came up to her neck in a scoop and reached nearly to her knees. Under it was a pair of black leggings and she had her feet tucked into a pair of sheepskin moccasins. My eyes kept drifting back to the sweater and how it hugged her hips and bottom. She glanced over and caught me staring. I held her eyes, refusing to look away and make her think I didn't like what I saw.

"So, do you like Cornish game hens?" she asked, shutting off the water.

"I've never had one, actually. I'm guessing they taste like chicken?" I joked and she snorted.

"Yup, just like chicken. Hopefully, mouthwatering, delicious chicken. I have a wonderful recipe from Garrett for rosemary and garlic hens," she explained, setting the washed birds on a paper towel and moving around the kitchen like she belonged there.

"Garrett is your roommate, right?" I asked and she nodded.

"That's right. He's head chef at Snowberry Falls."

I whistled low. "Head chef at the most elite country club in the area. You must love it when he brings home leftovers," I joked and she turned, a pan in her hand.

"I never turn down a meal, as you can see," she said, curtsying.

I set my mug down on the coffee table. "Why do you do that?" I asked.

She slid the pan onto the stove, adding the vegetables and birds she had already cleaned. "Do what?" She parroted, as though she didn't know what I was talking about.

"Make fun of your body. You did it in bed the other night, too," I pointed out and she washed her hands, obviously buying time as the water ran.

"I don't know why I do it. I guess because all of my life, I've been told that 34-24-34 is the place to be, and I'm so not," she explained embarrassedly, sliding the pan into the oven.

"I'm more of a 38-29-38 kind of guy." I winked and she stopped, one hand still on the oven door.

"That's so...." She motioned with her hand while I waited, but she came up with nothing.

"Refreshing?" I asked and she shrugged.

"Unusual, I guess," she admitted, walking towards me. She sat next to me on the couch and tucked one leg under her butt. "But enough about me, how are you feeling?"

"I'm good. The pain is gone and I only have a little weakness left. I'm quite surprised by it."

"We're lucky to have such a good surgeon like Dr. Brooks right in town. I'm glad he was able to help you and it improved your pain so quickly. I've been worried about you since you left the hospital on Monday."

Her hand was resting on the couch and I grasped it in mine. "You can call or text me anytime. I should have called you, but I was, I don't know. I didn't want to hear you weren't coming. I don't know what this is, but being there with you Sunday night was peaceful, and I liked how it made me feel."

She gazed down at our hands, already knotted together without any conscious effort. "I liked how it made me feel, too. I felt safe, and even though you were the one hurting, you made me feel like I was the most important person in the room. I don't feel that way often."

I reached up and tucked a long brown lock behind her ear. "You should feel that way. You're important to me. I'm glad you came over tonight, and not just because you're cooking." I winked and she blushed.

"I feel bad that all of this came up just when you were ready to start the new job." She leaned back against the couch a little to relax. "The hospital is pretty understanding, though. Did they give you more time off?"

"Is this your way of asking if they fired me?" I asked questioningly, and she leaned forward quickly.

"No, no, I just meant I hoped they didn't rescind the offer because of this. I stink at this making small talk thing." She leaned back against the couch again and closed her eyes, shaking her head a little.

I chuckled and rubbed her thigh for a second. I quickly removed my hand when I remembered that might be too familiar for this stage of the game. "I'm not much for small talk. I prefer to speak honestly with a woman. So, to answer your question, they didn't rescind the offer. I went there today and did the first part of the orientation." Her eyes popped open and her mouth fell open, ready to read me the riot act, but I held up my hand. "It was fine. I only went in for an hour to fill out paperwork and such. They postponed the longer orientation and broke it into two parts for next week. They also agreed to let me work part-time for a few weeks and ease into full-time as my back allows. They've been very understanding."

She rolled her head to the side and smiled. "Good. I'm not surprised, though. They want the best working at their hospital, and if that means they have to be flexible to avoid losing the best, then they bend over backward. I know it's still stressful for you."

I shrugged my shoulder. "To be honest, my whole life has been this way. It's always something, so you just figure out ways around whatever is happening at the time."

"Is that your way of telling me that dating a guy in a wheelchair isn't easy?" she asked, a little hesitantly.

"That's not what I meant at all. I meant that my life has always been about one step forward and two steps back. As long as you brought it up, though, I'll answer your question. No, it's not easy to date a guy in a wheelchair, for multiple reasons. The least of which is probably what you're thinking."

"And just what am I thinking?" she sparred with me.

I definitely met my match with this one.

"You're thinking, *am I dating a guy in a wheelchair?*"

She laughed with abandon and it reminded me of Sunny as she ran and played through the park on a Saturday afternoon.

"It's true, that's exactly what I was thinking because you're not a guy in a wheelchair to me. You're Jason Alexander, a really nice guy who took my breath away when he kissed me at my door the other night. You're the guy who, even after surgery, shared his bed with me, so I'd be comfortable. You're the guy who lets his heart be ruled by a four-year-old and doesn't even care. You're a guy sitting on the couch next to me who I really want to kiss if it wasn't inappropriate at the present time," she stammered.

I let go of her hand and cupped her face, guiding her toward me. I kept my eyes open, as hers went closed and I watched as her pink, sweet lips came toward mine. She sighed somewhere deep in her chest when our lips touched. Only then did I let my eyes close, and her arms came up around my neck. I held back, kissing her lips, but manipulating her body until she was plastered to my side, her head resting against the couch. I deepened the kiss then, letting my lips control hers. I loved the way she whimpered when I pulled her lower lip through my teeth at the end.

"You're so beautiful, December," I whispered, lowering my head again to finish what I started. The kiss was interrupted by a beeping from the kitchen.

She sighed and gave me an apologetic smile. "Sorry. We don't want dinner to burn."

I gave her a hand up and waited until she was back in the kitchen. When she wasn't looking, I glanced down at my pants, disturbed by what I didn't see.

Chapter Eight

"Garrett taught you well," I sighed from the couch. We had finished dinner and she was cleaning up the kitchen while I lounged, as she put it, on the couch.

"Thank you, but I actually could cook long before I met Garrett. My family owns a chain of restaurants, and I was cooking from an early age," she said nonchalantly, rinsing the pan she had baked the hens in.

"I had no idea. Your family owns a restaurant chain and you became a nurse?" I asked, surprised.

She dried her hands on the towel and hung it on the handle of the stove to dry. She joined me on the couch with the wine bottle and sank into the cushions with her leg tucked under her again. I raised my glass of wine to her. "To a good meal. Thank you for letting me stay when I showed up on your doorstep."

I brought my glass to my lips and watched as she did the same. It was obvious she didn't want to talk about her family, so rather than cause a rift, I changed the subject. "It's been my pleasure, really. You've cooked me a delicious meal and even

KATIE METTNER

brought great wine. I enjoy your company, December. What can I do for you?"

Her eyes widened and she choked slightly on her wine. "Nothing, I'm just enjoying the warm fire and your company. I was going to offer to massage your back if you'd like."

I set my glass on the table and took her hand. "That's nice of you to offer, but I can't sit here and take, take, take without giving. Maybe I could offer you a massage. Sunny says I'm pretty good at it." I waved my hands, but she shook her head.

"You're not massaging my back. You're the one who just had surgery," she insisted.

"You know, I'm really tired of everyone thinking I'm some delicate flower that needs constant coddling, so my petals don't flutter to the ground," I ground out, my frustration bubbling over. "I'm tired of being emasculated because I hurt my back. People hurt their damn backs every day." I closed my eyes and took a deep breath, knowing I needed to simmer down.

The couch shifted and I opened my eyes to see her slipping her coat on. She put her hand on the doorknob and I swung into Sport. "December, wait. I'm sorry, I'm frustrated. I didn't mean to take it out on you."

"I understand, Jay. I'll let you rest. Talk to you soon," she said without turning, and then pulled the door closed behind her.

KISS

I unlocked the wheels on my chair and backed out from behind my desk. My new office was nicely situated in a corner space with windows on two sides that looked out over the peace garden. The gardens were quiet this time of year as the weather grew colder.

I had finished my orientation last week and decided to spend a few days in the office, familiarizing myself with procedures and staff. It's a short week with Thanksgiving on Thursday, but that was helping me work into the position slowly.

Thursday would be a week since I'd been rude to December and she had left upset. I sent flowers and an apology but hadn't heard anything from her. I guess my big mouth, and the chip on my shoulder, screwed up what could have been a good thing. I'd spent every night since dreaming about how good her lips felt on mine.

I turned to the right and left a few times, trying to stretch out my back, something that was common lately as I recovered.

"Back bothering you?" a voice from the door asked and I looked up, surprised by the intrusion.

"December, hi." I smiled, wheeling Sport to where she stood against the doorframe. "Just a little stiff at the end of the day, no big deal. How are you?"

"I finished my shift and noticed a light on in

here. It's been a while since this office was filled. It's nice to see the light on and somebody home. I know the patients are going to benefit from having a full-time social worker again."

I tentatively reached for her hand that was hanging at her side. "I hope so. I also hope you forgive me for being a jack diggity last week. It was uncalled for, immature, and you didn't deserve that kind of treatment."

"Jack diggity?" She laughed a little but left her hand in mine.

"I'm terrible at swearing. I sound plain ridiculous, so one day, Sunny and I made up words we could use when we were mad that were safe. Jack diggity replaces, well, you can probably guess."

"I get the picture, yes. Also, there's nothing to forgive. I left because you were tired and needed to rest, but also because patients yell at me regularly at work. I tend to shy away from it in my personal life." She smiled and I nodded, knowing my eyes were guilt-ridden.

"Will you give me a second chance? I haven't quit dreaming about you since Thursday," I admitted, going with honesty.

She leaned down and kissed my lips, friendly and light, but it still left me burning. "You don't need a second chance, we just need to make time for another date. I've been working twelve-hour shifts for the last four days, that's why I didn't call. I'm headed home now to sleep for the next twenty-four hours."

I instantly accepted the olive branch she held out. "Do you have plans for Thanksgiving? We all go to my mom and dad's house for a big dinner with all the fixings. If you'd like to come, we'd love to have you."

She cocked her head to the right a little, "You want me to come to a family holiday?"

I nodded immediately. "My mom would love to meet the woman who rescued her baby and feed her turkey. It's what us Alexanders do."

She snorted with laughter and held up her hands. "Okay, with an invitation like that, I can't say no. I didn't really have any plans other than watching the parade since Garrett is going to pick up Sage at her mom's. I'd love to come and share the day with you."

I took her hand and kissed the back of it. "I'm thankful you stopped by. Let me walk you to your car." I winked and she laughed, following me out of the office.

KISS

I parked my truck in the garage stall and pocketed the key. After I left December at her Jeep, I stopped at the store for a few things and planned to stay in for the next day and rest my back, so I was in tip-top shape for Thursday. It was always a long and tiring day filled with food, laughter, and my nieces and nephews zooming around the house like zip lines trying to catch each other. Most years,

I'd be right in the middle of it, but not this year. I would have to be careful about how much rough-housing I did, so I could start work full-time next week.

"Are you getting out or living in there permanently?" a voice asked and I rolled my eyes. Dully hauled Sport from the back of the truck and set it on the ground, so I pushed the door open and used my hands to swing my legs out of the enclosure.

"I was thinking about Thursday and wondering if I should add another notch to my belt since I was in the garage," I joked, swinging into Sport and placing my feet on the footplate.

"Mom's cooking, of course, you should." Dully laughed, grabbing my briefcase and two bags of groceries from the car. "I'll carry these down for you."

I nodded, biting my tongue, so I didn't take his head off about helping me. *It's not a big deal to accept help from time to time,* I told myself. It just seemed like the last few weeks it had been non-stop. I twisted the key in the door to the cottage and held the door for him. He set the bags on the table and started putting the stuff away.

"Dully, I can put my own groceries away," I insisted, slinging my scarf over the wooden coat tree and dropping my hat over it.

"I know you can, but I wanted to talk to you anyway," he ruminated, slipping the two bottles of wine I'd bought onto the bottom shelf of the fridge.

Ut-oh, he wanted to talk. That usually meant I'd done something wrong. "You want to talk? Have I done something I shouldn't have?"

Dully shrugged, folding one bag into a perfect triangle. "You tell me."

I stared at him like he had four heads. "Last time I checked, everything was cool. Did I miss something?"

He grabbed two beers from the fridge and came over, settling in the chair. He handed me a beer and cracked his open. I set mine on the table and loosened my tie. I wanted to shower and get into some comfortable clothes, but he looked like he was here to stay. I cracked open my beer and took a long pull of the dark, smoky liquid. "This is about December, isn't it?" I asked, acutely aware he was watching me closely.

"Snow mentioned December left here upset the other night, or at least it seemed that way when she talked to her at work."

"I see, well, you can tell your wife that December and I are fine, and she's coming to Thanksgiving dinner," I informed him.

He sat forward quickly, almost spilling his beer. "Are you serious?"

"As serious as mom is when she's basting a forty-pound turkey at four a.m.," I quipped.

"Wow, I guess Snow was way off on this one," Dully mused.

I drank some more beer and tried to shrug off the feeling of knowing I was about to disappoint him. "No, she was right, at least up until about an hour ago."

Dully set his bottle down and folded his hands. It was the teacher pose that made me feel like I'd done something wrong. It made it hard to have a conversation with the man when I felt like I was about to get detention.

"Could you not do that?" I asked, motioning at his hands, "it makes you look so teacherish." He snorted and unfolded his hands, grabbing his beer and leaning back, letting his tongue fall to one side. "Much better."

"December did leave here upset the other night?" Dully asked, trying to prod me along.

"Yeah, I was a jack diggity and she was on the receiving end. I was frustrated with my situation and took it out on her. I apologized then, again with flowers, and again tonight, but she said she wasn't upset. She understood I was just frustrated."

"But you think she was upset?" Dully asked, and I nodded.

"I know she was, and I know it was wrong for me to be rude when she was trying to help," I admitted.

"What was she offering?" he asked, perplexed.

"A massage. She offered to massage my back for me because she used to work on a rehab floor and knew a lot about it. I told her I was tired of being coddled and she didn't need to pretend like I was a delicate flower." I shook my head at myself and he set his bottle down again.

"Did you not want a massage? Did your back hurt? I'm confused."

"We were having a nice time together. I offered to give her a massage because she'd been so nice and cooked dinner for me. She insisted that I should be the one getting the massage because I was the one who had surgery. I just kind of lost it and told her to quit treating me like a child," I said, ashamed.

His brows rose to the ceiling. "I think she was trying to be nice."

"She was, but I guess the stress built up over the last few weeks and I popped off. So not cool, I know. I was frustrated, but that doesn't make it okay," I admitted, and my voice was as contrite as I felt.

"What are you so frustrated about? The hospital has been understanding and held the job, you don't have to worry about moving, and you got a new chair. The surgery was a bump in the road, considering how quickly you've recovered."

I growled a little and ripped the tie off from around my neck. "I'm not completely healed and I don't know if I'll ever be. It's frustrating me, especially when December is around."

"I'll say it again. I'm confused." Dully picked up the tie I had tossed and untied it.

I stared off over his shoulder at the picture of us in the woods with our old dog, Jasper. "Not everything is working the way it was before the surgery," I said, my gaze dropping to my pants. I ran a hand through my hair and sighed. "When I kiss her, things don't happen the way they used to."

"Did they before the surgery?" he asked and I nodded.

"It was the one thing I had going for me as a disabled guy, and now I don't even have that," I sighed.

Dully waved his hand around in the air. "Wait a damn minute here, brother. Are you telling me you think the only thing you have to offer someone is the fact that your plumbing still works? Do I need to call the counselor and get you an appointment? I'm suddenly extremely concerned. You're so much more than your disability. Look at the job you just landed."

"No, you don't understand, Dul. I meant it's the one thing I had to offer a woman. If she's going to be with a guy like me and put up with the day to day hassles I create, then I want to at least keep her satisfied," I tried to explain.

Dully sat back in the chair and didn't say a word. He just sat there. I rolled Sport down the hall to my bedroom and pulled my suit coat off, throwing it on the bed, followed by my dress shirt and suit pants. He wasn't leaving soon, so for now, I'd have to find something more comfortable to wear and shower later.

I dug out my Vikings sweatshirt and a pair of grey jogging pants, tugging them over my hips and leaving my watch on the chest of drawers on the way out. When I rolled back into the room, he was in the same place.

"Does everything else work down there? Your bladder, etc.?" he asked before I was all the way back to the table. I diverted to the stove and preset the oven, so I could bake a pizza for dinner.

"Yes, it all works and everything feels the same. Except on our first date, every time I kissed her, my lower half was at attention. Thursday night, it never got out of bed. I felt the same inside, but nothing happened," I explained, feeling like a prepubescent boy in puberty education class.

"It hadn't even been a week since the surgery on Thursday. Did it occur to you that maybe your body just needed time to recover?" Dully asked softly.

"That's what I've been hoping, but so far, no dice. Thursday night, I was frustrated in general and probably shouldn't have had company. I'll do my best to make her feel really special at Thanksgiving. I know mom is going to love her," I said over my shoulder, sliding the pizza into the oven and setting the timer.

I rolled my chair over to the table and picked up my beer, just as he set his down. "Jay, promise me we aren't going back to where we were three years ago. So help me God, I will drag your butt into the counselor's office if I think for a second that's what's going on."

I glanced up at his anxious face. "Dul, chill.

We aren't going anywhere but forward. You said it yourself, this surgery was just a bump in the road. I need to give myself more time and try to be less high strung about everything. I'm stressed, though. A new job is stressful, and I can't even work out to keep myself grounded. It's hard to admit I'm getting old," I joked.

He frowned instead of laughed and leaned forward to make eye contact. "If things aren't back to normal in a month after the surgery, promise me you'll call the doctor. Your surgery was higher up on the spine and wouldn't have any bearing on your lower extremity function. Changes in that area might mean a change in your lower spine and that should be looked at," he insisted and I put my hands up.

"Okay, I promise. If things aren't looking up, I'll call." I laughed at my play on words and he rolled his eyes.

He got up and set his empty beer bottle on the sink before opening the front door. "And just for the record, being able to please December in bed isn't going to be the only reason she stays with you. I'm married to a disabled woman who's in a chair all the time, and our relationship has nothing to do with how satisfied she keeps me in bed. I hope someday you'll understand that being with a woman, disabled or not, is not about your body, but about your heart."

Chapter Nine

"I'm so stuffed," December groaned, squeezing my hand as we strolled down the paved path through the woods from my parents' house.

We'd finished dinner a few hours ago, and December helped my mom and sister clean up dishes and pack up to-go packages of food. A paper bag of recycled butter dishes and cottage cheese containers swung at December's side as she walked. She came dressed in soft jeans and a grey Minnesota Vikings sweatshirt and looking sexy as anything I'd ever seen. I spent the meal with one hand on her lap, loving how soft the jeans were and how the heat radiated from her body into my hand.

As everyone began to disperse from the house, I invited December back to my cottage for a glass of wine. It was the least I could do to make up for last week.

"That's one great benefit of using a chair, I can unbutton my pants and they don't fall down." I winked and she snickered a little.

"It's also the benefit of having big hips. Mine are unbuttoned and you don't even know it." She laughed, only this laugh was more self-deprecating than humor.

"At the risk of getting slapped, I love how your hips feel under those jeans. I was having a hard time keeping my hands off them."

She gave me half a smile without actually making eye contact. "I noticed."

"Never be afraid to tell me to keep my hands to myself. I'm a touchy-feely kind of guy, and I know some people aren't."

She squeezed my hand again. "I'm usually the recipient of grabbing and groping, so I like touchy-feely." She stopped and gazed up at the sky as we broke into the opening between Dully's driveway and the path to my house. "It's so beautiful out here. Look at all the stars."

I stopped the chair and leaned my head back, letting the darkness of the night take over my soul. The stars twinkled against the big black canvas in a rhythm that lulled you into a sense of being a star yourself. They undulated in a random pattern that eventually became a dance among them.

"I've lived out here my whole life, and the stars have always been there for me. After surgeries or trips to the hospital, Mom would roll me out onto the deck, so I could stare at the stars. Often times, she'd lay me on a chaise lounge and bundle me up so I could stay there for an hour or more. I dreamed one day I could fly up there with those stars, just me, without the chair, and be free. When I fell asleep, Dully would carry me to bed and I'd wake in the morning sad that I wasn't with the stars," I whispered.

She squeezed my shoulder. "I can't imagine what it was like to be a kid trapped in a chair and not understand why."

I shrugged the shoulder she held. "I never let myself get frustrated in front of my mother," I admitted. "She always carried so much guilt about it as it was. I couldn't take my frustrations out on her."

She slipped her hand in mine and started walking again, down the short path to the ramp to my deck. I motioned for her to go first and followed behind her, watching the swing of her hips with each step, another rhythm I could watch all night. She held the door open and I rolled through.

She set the bag on the floor and took off her coat, hanging it on the coat tree as though she was a frequent guest in my home. I loved that she was comfortable enough to make herself comfortable. She took the bag into the kitchen and began to pull containers from it, setting them on the counter.

"Your mom feels guilty because you have spina bifida?" she asked, almost as though it just finally dawned on her.

"Yes, she always has. She says had she known she was pregnant, she would have gotten care earlier." I rolled to the small kitchen island and pulled two glasses from the shelf and took the bottle of wine from her outstretched hand.

She put the containers in the fridge and then grabbed the corkscrew and followed me to the living room. I lit the fire I had readied earlier and swung onto the couch, happy to sink into the soft cushions after a long day in the chair.

"She knows that neural tube defects can't always be prevented, even if the mother takes the recommended amount of folic acid, right? There is research to suggest that some embryos don't metabolize the folic acid correctly and that is the reason for the defect. It isn't anything a woman does to her child," she said empathetically.

I nodded and held out my hand in a shrug. "That's the thing, she was taking folic acid the entire time. She may not have known she was pregnant with me, but she was still taking her prenatal vitamin because it had only been a year since my brother, Bram, was born. Maybe it's just a mom thing, you feel like you failed before you even got started."

"Maybe. I certainly can't pass judgment, I'm not a mother, but I feel terrible that she carries guilt she doesn't need to." She sipped her wine and I half-nodded, half-shrugged.

"Believe me, I do, too. I think it's what drives me to be successful. I want her to see that the chair doesn't keep me from living a full life." I motioned at the chair and her head tilted a little. "I know, that sounds bad, doesn't it? I just mean I'm trying to give her some peace." I sipped my wine to give my brain time to catch up with my mouth.

"I get it. My father died when I was a freshman in high school, and my mother carried around this guilt that she had pushed him into an early grave with the business. It had been her idea to expand the business a few years before he died."

"Did he die of a heart attack or something?" I asked, and she shook her head.

"No, he died of lung cancer from smoking. That's why we all told her he made his own bed," she explained, pouring some more wine in her glass.

"She wasn't forcing him to smoke the cancer sticks," I pointed out. "That was his decision, business or no business."

"We could see that, but she said he would have smoked less if he hadn't been so stressed out. It's the typical game of *what if* everyone plays when they lose their rock. Life became one big battle to keep what she saw was our father's legacy." She tipped the rest of the glass back and drained it, setting it on the coffee table. "Anyway, enough about me."

I shook my head and held up my hand. "No, continue. You know everything about me, and I know hardly anything about you. Did your dad know you didn't want to work in the family business?"

"He did. I told him when he was dying that it was my dream to help people, and not by bringing them a piece of pie and coffee. I wanted to be a nurse. He confided in me it wasn't his dream for me, or my brother, to keep the family business alive. He made me promise I would never let my mother guilt me into feeling like I had to. He wanted me to follow my dreams and be my own person. He knew just how hard that was going to be when it came to my mother." She picked up the bottle of wine and went to pour, but then thought better of it.

"Go ahead, have another glass," I encouraged.

"I have to drive home," she said slowly.

"You're more than welcome to stay over, either here, or if you're more comfortable, up at Snow and Dully's, but I do have a guest room." I smiled and she smiled, a little relieved.

"I might be a little too comfortable here, to be honest. I really like this little cottage, and I really like you. Too much more alcohol and I'll be saying things I shouldn't."

I picked up the bottle and poured the dark burgundy wine into her glass, then handed it to her. "Relax. I'm not going to bite, and I love that you're comfortable here. I like you, December, a lot. I won't lie about that. I also would never take advantage of you, not that I could."

Her glass lowered to her leg slowly. "What does that mean?"

I groaned a little and twirled the wine glass in my hand. "Things aren't exactly working the greatest since surgery." I grimaced. "I can't believe I'm even telling you this."

She rested her hand on my leg. "Did things work great before surgery?"

I nodded, the heat on my cheeks obvious to her

as she sat staring at me. "Yeah, I'm lucky my lesion is low and I still have feeling in my pelvis."

She nodded once. "I noticed on your chart."

I groaned again. "That's right, you took care of me in recovery. This might be my worst nightmare."

"Jay, I didn't peek if that's what you're worried about," she assured me. "I just noticed that you didn't have a catheter and that you didn't need one."

"I'm completely dying of embarrassment right now," I groaned.

She took my hand, linking her fingers in mine. "Why?"

"Because I really like you, December, and before the surgery, everything worked. Now, it doesn't. I'm a guy and that's important. I'm worried that maybe it's a complex or something and I've never, you know, been with a woman. I'm frustrated because I really like you," I said again, closing my eyes and banging my head a few times on the couch.

"I really like you, too, Jay. How much I like you has nothing to do with what parts do and don't work on your body, and I'm not just talking about your legs. You have to remember the surgery was only a few weeks ago, and your body needs time to recover. It could be a month or six weeks before your body decides it has the energy to share with the rest of your systems that aren't absolutely necessary for survival. The body is amazing that way.

I don't think it's a complex. I think you just need to relax."

I rubbed my free hand on my thigh. "That's what Dully said, too. He said I should give it at least a month."

"He's right. Don't feel pressured because you think I expect something from you. I don't. I just want your back to heal right. If down the road, you still feel like you need help in other departments, I'd be happy to go with you to the clinic," she offered and I swallowed my wine slowly.

"You would?" I was definitely in the twilight zone.

"I would. If we've taken our relationship in a direction that is serious enough to consider making love, then our relationship, at least for me, is serious enough to be there for every aspect of each other's lives. I take giving myself to someone very seriously. In fact, well, I have never actually felt serious enough about anyone to have taken that step yet."

She muttered the last sentence and I had to tip her chin up to hold her eyes. "You're a virgin, too?"

She nodded, biting her lip and rolling her eyes upward a little bit. "Yes, I'm a twenty-five-year-old virgin. Not that I haven't had offers, I just. I don't know. I just…"

"Respect yourself enough to know that giving yourself to someone completely is important and worth waiting for?" I asked and her face calmed a bit.

"Exactly like that." She smiled, taking a sip of wine.

"Dully will be relieved," I said, setting my wine down.

"Was he worried that I was going to walk away or something? I hope I don't give off that kind of vibe."

I shook my head and took her hand. "No, he was worried I was falling back into a situation I went through back when I was in college."

She squeezed my hand and gave me an encouraging smile. "Will you tell me what it is?"

"It's a long story and I don't want to bore you with it."

She shrugged. "I have all night."

I sighed and she rested my hand on her thigh while she listened. "I was a freshman in college and I lived there during the week and came home on the weekends. I was lonely, wasn't making any friends, and had a really big crush on a girl who was way out of my league. That Christmas, I was home for break and Dully proposed to Snow. They were so happy, and that gave me hope maybe someday I'd find a woman who didn't care about my chair, the way Dully didn't care about Snow's."

I took a breath and she threw her leg over mine, straddling my thighs. She leaned in until our foreheads were touching.

"For the record, I don't care about the chair, either," she whispered, laying her head on my shoulder and hugging me carefully.

I brought my arms around her and held her lightly, enjoying the way she fit in between the muscles of my chest perfectly. "You need to understand the differences I have from most men, December. I will have issues that come up for the rest of my life."

She sat up and took my face in her hands. "I understand them completely, Jay. My career has taken me down some pretty interesting paths and I have had some enlightening experiences. I might be young, but I have a unique perspective most people my age don't. I don't see the chair. I see this incredibly gorgeous man, who shouldn't have looked twice at me. He's got muscles everywhere, eyes to get lost in, and soft, wavy locks that slide through your fingers. When he wears a suit, I want to be the one holding his hand at dinner, and when he's in jeans and a sweatshirt, I want to be the one he's holding on the couch. That's my perspective."

She leaned in and guided my mouth to hers, her lips warm and sweet from the wine. She plied my lips with her warmth, running her tongue over them, heating and wetting them until I dropped my jaw and granted her access. She sighed and her tongue darted in to explore mine. I angled my head to go deeper and taste the sweetness of her more.

I lightened the kiss, pulling back slowly while we both breathed heavily. "You're incredible," I whispered against her lips.

"I've never felt like this before," she whispered back.

"Me either," I admitted.

She laid her head on my shoulder and patted my chest. "I'm sorry for interrupting. Go on with your story."

"I feel really good right now, do I have to?" I asked.

She shook her head a little. "No, you don't. We don't have to talk at all if you don't want to. I'm happy to just lay here with you."

I leaned back against the couch pillow, being careful not to twist my back, and she swung her hips over my lap. I rested my head on hers, thankful for the reprieve from telling her the most shameful moment of my life. I may have come to terms with it, but telling others about it left me open to criticism I wasn't sure I could handle, especially from her.

Her body relaxed against my chest with every breath and soon, she was breathing slow and even.

This woman who was quickly stealing my heart had fallen asleep on my chest, and I would do anything to keep her there all night.

Chapter Ten

December

"Jay, wake up." I shook him gently, but his arms were wrapped around me tightly. "Jay, come on, you can't sleep out here all night," I whispered.

I struggled within his grasp for a few seconds and he jumped awake. "Don't leave," he slurred, his voice frantic.

I rested my hand on his chest. "I'm not leaving, I just want you to go to bed. It's not good for your back to sleep out here."

He rubbed his hand over his face for a second. "I am a little sore. Good call."

I helped him sit up and maneuvered Sport next to the couch. He transferred in gingerly and I followed him down to his bedroom. The clock read two fifty-eight a.m. and that meant we'd been asleep for nearly four hours. My car was still parked at his mother's house and I was going to have to leave here in the morning under their watchful eye. I sighed a little out of resignation and pulled back the bedspread. His room was done in rich rustic tones that complemented the space, and the man.

I smoothed the sheets and he transferred to the bed.

"Let me massage the tight spots so you can fall back to sleep," I encouraged, sitting on the edge of the bed.

"I'm going to take you up on that, strictly platonic, of course." He grinned sleepily.

I helped him get comfortable on his side and used pillows to prop his legs, then went to work on the knotted muscles.

"Oh, that feels good, December," he moaned, his body relaxing a little as I kneaded his spine.

"I learned massage as a way to put myself through college. You wouldn't believe how many people are wound up tighter than a drum," I joked, tickling his neck a little.

"Your dad didn't leave you money for school?" he asked, his tone surprised.

"He did, without telling my mom. We had a falling out when the will was read and I refused to take any money from her after that. I decided it would be better not to be beholden to the family. Know what I mean?" I laughed a little and he tensed immediately under my hands.

"I guess I'm really beholden to my family then," he admitted in a monotone voice.

I stopped massaging and crawled over him, lying on my side to face him. "No, Jay, my situation is completely different. You don't worry about anyone in your family holding it over your head, do you?" I asked and he shook his head no. "I do. If

I had taken the money, they would have tried to control my life."

He reached out and tucked a hair behind my ear. "That's hard, babe. I'm sorry they're like that. My family saved my life. I owe them everything."

His face turned ashen as some memory pulled him back in time.

"Saved your life literally or figuratively?" I asked the weight of his pain heavy on my chest.

"Literally," he sighed, his hand reaching to fix the pillow behind his back.

"Is this what you were trying to tell me about earlier?"

He rested his hand on my hip and nodded grimly. "Yeah, I don't like to talk about it. It's not my proudest moment."

I rubbed his cheek tenderly and smiled warmly. "You don't have to tell me, but I won't judge you."

He held my eyes and whatever he saw in them must have been enough for him.

"Like I said, it was the year Dully proposed to Snow. I was coming home on the weekends for tux fittings and to get to know Snow better. I had this huge crush on a girl at college and was trying to figure out how to ask her out. She was a cheerleader, you know, your typical college sorority girl. She acted interested in me and Dully encouraged me to ask her out for Valentine's Day. She accepted and that night, I went to pick her up at her friend's house," which he put in air quotes, "but it turned out to be an empty lot."

I had sadness for that boy as I gazed into his eyes. "She stood you up. I'm so sorry."

He half-shrugged. "I drove past her house and saw her there kissing some other guy, and I just kept driving. It was a few days later when I found out she agreed to the date because she wanted to find out what it was like to do it with a crippled guy, but chickened out at the last minute. She said she was afraid it would be too creepy and awkward."

I leaned in and kissed his lips gently. "She's wrong. I'm sorry. I'm embarrassed to be a woman right now."

He smiled a little and held my face with his hand. "I know now that not all women are like her, but back then, I was crushed. I was embarrassed and horrified that my sexual abilities were being discussed in that way around campus. I drove home a few weeks later and stayed at my mom's. I decided it would be the last time I would see them all. I hadn't gone back to class and I was ready to end it. End all the struggling, the pain, the embarrassment, the horror, all of it. I kissed my mother goodbye and waved at Dully, just like I always did, as I pulled out of the driveway.

I didn't know how I was going to do it, and I drove on autopilot thinking about how I was going to miss Dully's wedding and miss out on meeting his babies. I was crying by the time I hit the outskirts of Winona. I knew I needed help, but I didn't have anyone to turn to at school."

I wiped a tear off his face and he took my hand, pressing a kiss into my palm.

"You don't have to go on," I started to say, but he shook his head.

"I want to tell you. I want you to know." He waited and I nodded for him to continue. "I turned around and started driving back to Dully's. I needed to tell him what had happened. I didn't have a solution, but I couldn't go back to school. I don't know where I was on the ride back, but it started snowing lightly and the road had ice on it. I lost control of the truck and went off the road. The truck flew through a field and when I tried to gain control, it flipped over, coming to a stop on the roof in a pile of snow." He stopped speaking and squeezed my hand. "Would you get me some water?"

I sat up instantly. "Sure, just give me a second," I promised, climbing off the bed and leaving the bedroom. I wanted to give him a few moments to collect himself, so I wandered to the kitchen and got a bottle of water for each of us. I also grabbed a plate of cookies his mom had sent home with us and carried it all back to his room. I went around the bed and handed him a bottle, which he took gratefully. I set the cookies and my bottle on the bedside table then sat back down on the bed. He took a long swig of the water and then screwed the cap back on, drumming his fingers on it.

"Thanks, the turkey made me thirsty."

I picked up the plate of cookies. "Cookie? They look great, but I didn't have room after dinner."

He laughed and shook his head. "No, I'll pass. My mommy always scolded me about leaving crumbs in the bed."

"Ah, yes, the ghost of mother past." I set the plate down and took a drink of my own water. "So, you left off with your truck upside down."

He nodded once. "I was upside down, too. Obviously, that put me in an awkward position since I can't just climb out and walk for help. I couldn't reach my phone because it had fallen out of the holder I kept it in. I figured I was going to die in that field and after I cried for ten minutes, I realized a notebook had been tossed around in the crash and was within reach. An hour later I was still hanging upside down, but I had started writing down all the things I should have said to everyone when I had the chance. I was sore and cold and certain I was going to die. It was dark, and I couldn't even see what I was writing, but it didn't matter. I was pouring out all the pain and heartache I dealt with on that paper. Every so often, my phone would ring, and then, slowly, it rang more frequently. It stopped ringing for a moment and would start right back up again. In a way, it was like a torture device laying there out of reach, trapped by my wheelchair tires, but in a way, it was a beacon of hope. Someone was trying to reach me and I wasn't answering. You know?"

I nodded and rubbed his shoulder. His arm was

covered in goosebumps and I pulled the blanket up over him. "Someone knew you should be answering that phone."

It was his turn to nod, and he sighed. "I don't know how long it was, probably a couple hours, but eventually, a bright light filled the rear window of the truck. If I hadn't been so cold and sore, I would have thought it was the light." He grinned a little and I chuckled, trying to keep the tears at bay. "It was a light. A big spotlight. The light didn't waver and pretty soon, I heard shouting and footsteps running toward the truck. A face appeared at the window and it was Dully screaming my name. The light was his deer shining light, and my brothers and dad were surrounding my truck. They knocked the window out and Dully crawled in next to me, keeping me warm until an ambulance arrived. I sat there in my truck and cried in his arms. I had never been happier to see his face in my life."

"I can only imagine," I whispered.

"They took me to the hospital and treated me for hypothermia, keeping me overnight to make sure my spine wasn't damaged. Dully stayed with me the whole night and I told him everything. I told him I didn't want to go back to school because now I knew I could never kill myself, but I also couldn't deal with facing the ones who had hurt me."

"This story is breaking my heart, Jay. I know this happens a lot to people with special circumstances, and I hate it every single time I hear about it. I hate this for you." I sighed and he wiped away the one tear I couldn't hold back.

"People with special circumstances?" he asked and I nodded.

"I don't like to use disabled or handicapped, because you aren't. You're a person with special circumstances. I've never met a person with special circumstances who don't have a way to overcome them, so I refuse to use disabled."

"You really are an old soul, you know that?" he asked and I shrugged. I knew it was true, my father told me that long ago.

"So, what happened? Obviously, you got your degree," I prodded.

"I was no worse for the wear, at least physically, so they sent me home the next morning. Dully got me settled at my mom's house, and then disappeared for a few hours. They had towed my truck back and when he walked in the door again, he had my chair and a new plan for me. I was a freshman, so most of my classes were available online. Dully organized with the college for me to do that while I recovered." He smirked and I giggled a little. Obviously, Dully had a way of getting people to come around to his way of thinking. "The next person to roll through the door was Snow. She and I talked for a long time that day. She confided in me that she had thought about killing herself several times during college. She said the stress of it all and the frustration of being different was sometimes more than she wanted to deal with, but she knew she had to keep going. I mean, look at what would have happened if she had ended her life," he said gesturing towards Sport, and I sucked in a deep breath.

"You're right, and I know someday you are going to have that same kind of impact on someone, Jay."

He kissed my hand, still twined in his. "I hope so, but it took me a long time to get there. I spent the next couple of semesters doing my courses online, seeing a counselor, and spending a lot of time with Snow and Dully. It ended up being a blessing in disguise because I finished all my freshman and sophomore college classes in half the time than if I had been in a classroom."

"Really?" I asked, surprised.

"Yeah, I guess self-paced just worked for me and I burned through the coursework. That left me with a bigger problem, though. I was now done with as much as I could do online and had to go back to school. I had a scholarship with St. Mary's and wasn't willing to give that up because someone thought they were better than me, so I sucked it up and went back. I was surprised when everyone started inviting me to functions and asking me to go to games with them. At first, I thought they were doing it out of charity, but I gave them a chance and it turned out they wanted to be my friend. My friend, Jonathan, was a model for a shirt company and brought me with him to an audition once. That was how I got into modeling. The girl who stood me up dropped out of college when she got pregnant, by the way."

I laughed and shook my head. "I guess you could say she got what was coming to her."

"In more ways than one, actually. Her son was born with several birth defects, including club feet. I have to give her credit, though. She rose to the occasion and is a great mom. She brought him to school one day and we talked. She apologized to me, and I accepted it and forgave her. I told her now we had freed each other and that meant we could be friends. We're still friends to this day."

"Really? A lot of people wouldn't be that forgiving, Jay. I probably wouldn't have been," I admitted.

"I'm not wasting my second chance by holding grudges. I helped her get back into school with an online academy and she married her son's daddy. It all turned out okay for her, and I'm glad. She was young and stupid, and I realize now it was all a lesson for me. A lesson in learning to deal with how people perceive us and how we don't have to let those perceptions define who we are. That was the reason I started modeling. I saw it as a way to show others that people in wheelchairs are the same as everyone else. We want the same things out of life, even if we have to ask for help occasionally."

He winked and I chuckled. "You do have a thing about asking for help. I understand why, though."

He glanced down at our hands twined together, and took a deep breath. "Whew, I've never told anyone outside of my family all of that before."

"Thank you for sharing it with me. I don't think two people can have a truly honest and open relationship if we hold back pivotal events in our life. They shape us and it's important to share those events with each other, so we can understand where each other is coming from."

"You're one of the most intuitive women I've ever met, you know that?" he asked, leaning down and kissing me softly.

"Well, if that's the case, my intuition is telling me you're exhausted and need to rest. I'll sleep in the guest room, so I don't bother you." I rolled to my knees, but he wouldn't let go of my hand.

"Stay, please? I'll be honest, when you fell asleep on me earlier, I'd never felt that peaceful before. I just want to feel you in my arms."

I reached over and flipped the switch on the side table next to him and the room was bathed in a soft light from the moon outside the window. "I fell asleep earlier because you make me feel safe. Is there anything I can do to make you more comfortable?" I asked, trying to arrange his pillows a little better.

He grabbed my wrist and pulled me down next to him until I was snuggled into him, my head on the pillow. He pulled the comforter over us and rested his hand on my belly. "Now I'm comfortable," he whispered, and I patted his hand on my stomach.

It wasn't long until I heard his soft, even breathing.

I closed my own eyes but I couldn't sleep. My intuition was too busy telling me things about my feelings regarding Jay Alexander.

Chapter Eleven

Jay

"Happy Birthday to my favorite nurse," I sang, kissing December's cheek.

"Jay, what a surprise!"

She smiled happily when I rolled into the nurse's station.

"It's your birthday. What's the surprise?" I asked, laughing.

"I didn't expect to see you since I'm working."

I took her hand and winked at the head nurse. "I know you're working, but I'm taking you for a lunch break."

She glanced behind her as I tugged her toward the elevator. "But…"

"It's quiet, December. Take an extra half an hour. We'll be fine." Teresa insisted then waved as we stood by the elevator.

"Okay, but text me if you get busy," she said as the elevator dinged and I pulled her in.

The doors slid shut and she stood in front of my chair, holding my hands. "Did you just steal me away from my work?"

I tugged her towards me, pulling her hands to

my legs until her lips were within kissing distance. "I did, and now I'm going to give you a birthday kiss."

She willingly leaned in and kissed me back, my hands coming up to capture her neck and angle her into me better. She was just about to climb on my lap when the elevator dinged and she jumped away, straightening her shirt as though her father was standing outside the door.

I pulled her out of the elevator and she stopped short, glancing around. "Wrong floor, Jay. The cafeteria is a few floors down."

I turned Sport enough to raise a brow at her. "I know where the cafeteria is, but I'm not taking you to the cafeteria for your birthday. That would be a punishment, not a gift."

She laughed freely, agreeing with a shake of her head. "That's true, but we don't really have time to go anywhere else," she fretted.

I motioned her to follow me and stopped at my office door. I unlocked it, hearing her short intake of breath at the sight in front of her. I rolled in and she followed, pushing the door shut behind her.

"Jay, this is..." she paused and I turned toward her, just in time to see her eyes welling with tears, "the nicest thing anyone has ever done for me."

She hung her head to hide her tears, but I heard her voice crack. I locked the chair and called her to me. "Come here, babe." I motioned for her to sit on my lap, but she shook her head.

"I don't want to hurt you."

"You won't, I promise. Sit on my lap and swing your legs over the wheel. I need to hold you."

She did as I asked and laid her head on my shoulder. I wrapped my arms around her and held her tightly, sneaking a kiss against her lips. "No one's ever surprised you on your birthday?"

She sighed and wiped her eyes. "No, birthdays were like any other day in our family. We spent them at the restaurant. After my father died, we never celebrated anything anymore. I've never had a birthday party. When I left home, I tried to change that, but it never worked out."

"What do you mean?" I asked, confused.

"I tried to acknowledge my brother's birthday for several years, and he returned the cards un-opened," she explained sadly.

I sighed, thinking back to what she had told me over Thanksgiving about her family. She had a falling out with her mother when she refused to stay and work in the business. They had a fight and her mother died shortly after. Her brother blamed her for her mother's death and bought out her half of the business, so he didn't have to consult her any longer about business decisions. They hadn't spoken since their mother's funeral.

It was easy to see how much she longed for a family. When we were at my parents' on Thanksgiving, she soaked up the happiness and love in the house. She spent hours talking to my mom and Snow and learned how to make some of the trad-itional family recipes between playing cards with my nieces. It didn't take me but a few moments to see she needed womanly comfort more than she needed me, so I stayed on the outskirts of the room.

"I wanted to be a special part of your day, even though you had to work. I know you volunteered to work on your birthday so Judy could spend the day with her daughter on hers."

She shrugged. "It's just another day to me, but kids are different. I didn't want Judy to miss her baby's first birthday."

"I love you, do you know that?" I asked softly and she froze in my arms. My breath hitched in my chest, too.

"You what?" she asked, her voice breathy.

I cleared my throat and licked my lips. I could see she was scared, but there was no going back now. "I love you. I'm sorry, I didn't mean to scare you, but it's true. Is that okay?" I asked, rubbing my thumb down her cheek.

"It's been a long time since anyone told me they loved me. I'm glad it was you." She smiled, rolling her eyes towards the ceiling a little. "That sounded lame. I'm really bad at this."

Her hand was holding her forehead and I pulled it down to rest in mine. "No, you're not. You're honest and real, and those are some of the other things I love about you. I know we haven't known each other very long, but I don't even question if I'm in love with you. I am. I just know. I've known since the first time we met. I didn't plan to tell you yet, it just slipped out. I don't want to scare you, but now that I've said it, I won't take it back. You don't have to say it back or feel awkward about it. I'm just telling you how I feel, and I understand you may not feel the same. I love spending time with you and talking for hours. I love laughing with you and watching really bad Bruce Willis movies together. I also love holding you against me and knowing you would never hurt me. You might as well know, if we spend any more time together, I'm going to be hard-pressed to let you go from my life."

She ran a hand down the side of my face and smiled, her eyes shining. "I could never hurt someone I love."

I hugged her to me, kissing the tender skin on her neck. It may not have been an open declaration of love, but I'd take it. She leaned back enough to find my lips and held the back of my head as she angled hers to get closer. She whimpered when I caught her lower lip between my teeth and her mouth opened when I tugged. I dove back to her lips and slipped my tongue in, losing myself in her. She bit down gently on it, her chest heaving against mine for a few seconds before she released me and let me twine my tongue with hers. She was so hot and sweet, I wanted nothing more than to lay her down and make love to her, but I couldn't. I couldn't until she was ready to give herself to me, and she wasn't.

I ended the kiss slowly and sighed. "We should

eat before you have to go back to work."

She climbed off my lap and straightened her scrubs shirt out. Today's was covered in Hello Kitty, and I couldn't help but smile at how cute she was. I held out the chair for her opposite my desk, which was now covered in candles, a bottle of sparkling cider, and fluted goblets.

"My, you have gone all out." She smiled and I popped the cork from the cider to pour some in her glass.

"You only turn twenty-six once," I reminded her. "How does it feel to be an old woman?" I asked introspectively, and she laughed, punching me playfully.

"I guess you'll find out in a few months, and then you can tell me what it's like to be an old man."

"Oh, you do know how to hit a guy below the belt." I laughed, rolling to the small box in the corner and pulling out our dinner. I set the box on my lap and rolled back.

"You got Gallo's? I love their bacon cheeseburger pizza." She raised a brow, rubbing her hands together.

I flipped the lid to reveal the contents and she squealed. "I think I oughta marry you." She winked and I laughed, serving a piece to her and then myself.

"Nothing makes me happier than to see you this happy. Let's eat and then I'll give you your birthday present." I picked up my slice and took a bite.

She picked hers up, bringing it to her mouth, but she stopped before she took a bite. "You got me a birthday present?"

I chewed and swallowed quickly. "Of course, it's your birthday."

She motioned around the office. "This is more than enough, really." Her hand went to the flowers in the vase next to her. "You even got narcissus, that's December's flower."

I nodded. "Savannah told me. I'd never seen them before, but she special ordered them for me."

She laid her hand over her chest. "That was so sweet of you. I love how they have a secret hidden center that's a different color than the petals. I feel that way sometimes. Like the face I show to the world is just covering up who I really am in my secret center."

She took a bite of her pizza and then her eyes went wide, clearly thinking about what she had just said. She waved her hand while she chewed and then sputtered. "I didn't mean it like that, not at all. I just meant…"

I took her hand and laid it down on the table. "I know what you meant, love. You meant people think they know you because of what they see on the surface, but in your heart, there is so much more."

"Yeah, exactly. This is great pizza. Thank you for going to so much bother for me." She took another bite and I leaned over my desk.

"Sweetheart, you're not a bother. I live to make you as happy as you make me."

She beamed as she devoured the first piece and I put a second on her plate.

"How has your first week been here at work?" she asked.

"It's been great. Everyone is always helpful and they're happy to have a social worker again."

"It's one of those cases of you don't realize what you have until you don't have it anymore. You guys have so much dropped on your desk all the time. I don't know how you get it all done," she pondered, her fingers caressing a flower petal.

"I feel the same way about what it must be like to be a nurse. I guess it's all about what our natural talents are. Lindsey came in earlier and brought a new project idea. I'm really excited about it." I sat back in Sport and she wiped her hands on her napkin.

"What kind of project? Isn't your job about finding nursing home beds and such?" she asked.

"Part of it is, yes. The other part is about community relations, education, and pretty much anything else the hospital needs at any given time. In this case, they need someone to take over their fundraiser calendar."

"I wondered if they were going to do that this year. The other nurses said we usually get an email by October and we've heard nothing." She was animated as she sat across from me now that our lunch was eaten.

"The previous social worker apparently was the one who started it, but it's so popular they want to continue it. In the past, they've done nature photography, but this year I'm thinking about going a different route." I watched her face, but she only lifted a brow and waited. "Since I've been a model, I have a lot of contacts in the business. This year's calendar is going to be a photoshoot of kids from our community with spinal cord disease or injury, doing everyday things. I'll be in some of the pictures, too, and I think it's going to be a lot of fun. Hopefully, it will inspire other people with special circumstances to not limit themselves because of their chairs."

"Jay, I think that's the best idea I've heard this year. The kids are going to love getting a taste of modeling, and you're right, so many others will benefit. Usually, the money raised from the calendars goes to a charity?" she asked, and I nodded.

"A foundation or research project gets the proceeds from the event, but this year I'm bringing something else to the table."

She motioned with her hand. "Like?"

"My proposal suggests the money go toward a barrier-free playground at the elementary school. The playground is also a city park and there are plenty of kids in the school, and the community, who would finally get a chance to play like real kids, if we could raise the funds."

Her hands were at her mouth and she was nodding, her eyes filled with tears. "Yes, and Dully will buy two dozen calendars, I'm sure. Providence is so lucky to have you. So am I." She smiled and I wheeled around the desk and took her hands in mine.

"We're running out of time together, so promise me you'll spend the weekend with me. I want to treat you to a real birthday dinner," I begged.

She nodded and leaned in for a kiss. "I think this is the birthday dinner I will never forget, though. I can't tell you how much this means to me."

"I was being a little selfish bringing you down here. I wanted you alone for a few minutes, but now I have to take you back." I reached under Sport and pulled out a small box, wrapped in snowflake paper. "But first, happy birthday, December."

She took the box from my hand and smiled, turning it over a couple times before she tore open one corner, her face in deep concentration. She pulled the lid off and gasped. "Jay, this is beautiful," she said on an exhale. She lifted it out of the box and the length of it fell from her fingers.

"It's a badge holder. I figured when it comes to nursing, practicality is in order. I saw a necklace like it in a little shop and asked them to make one into a badge holder."

"It's turquoise. That's one of the gemstones for December. Oh, look!" she exclaimed, her fingers caressing one of the small silver snowflakes. She put it around her neck and pulled her other one off, unclipping her badge and hooking it to the new one.

"I love it, Jay. You've made me so happy." She threw her arms around me in a hug.

"No happier than you make me every time we're together," I promised, kissing the soft spot behind her ear.

"I love you, Jason Alexander," she whispered so softly I almost didn't hear her, almost.

KISS

My hotel room was warm and I sat by the window watching the snow fall from the sky. It had started coming down during the meeting and instead of slacking off, it was intensifying with each hour. This afternoon, I drove down to meet with a friend of mine who had offered to do the calendar shoot pro bono for the exposure.

The weatherman promised the storm wouldn't arrive until tomorrow, but once again, he was wrong. When I left the meeting, I sat in my truck debating what to do, and a text from Dully came in. He was warning me that Highway 14 was covered in ice and snow, which meant the interstate would be, too. I promised him I'd stay over and drive home in the daylight.

It was the right decision because driving in the city was treacherous, I couldn't imagine what the highway must be like. The first snowfall of the season was usually as much ice as snow, and being upside down in a snowbank once in my life was enough. My phone rang and I rolled my chair the short distance to where it sat on the bed.

"Hello," I answered, still distracted by the mesmerizing flakes.

"Jay? Are you okay?" December asked worriedly.

"Hi, I'm fine, sweetheart. I was going to call, but didn't know when your break was. Dully suggested I stay overnight and I agreed. It's snowing hard here. How are you?" I asked, hoping she'd relax if she knew I was safe.

"I'm okay. I just agreed to stay for another shift in case the ER gets busy. It's likely with the first snow of the year," she lamented.

I chuckled. "You know it will be. You've worked a long shift already, though. I'm a little worried about you."

"I only worked an eight and I'll be resting in the on-call room. If they need me, they'll call, otherwise I'll just be chilling. I'd rather stay than be called in and have to come back on bad roads."

I blew out a breath. "I agree, but if you're too tired to drive home in the morning, call Dully. He'll come pick you up in the four-wheel drive and take you home. I'll be home sometime late morning. Okay?"

"I promise, though it would feel awkward to call him up and ask for a ride." She laughed but I could tell she wasn't kidding. I heard a beeping in the background. "Oh, I gotta go, first trauma is pulling in. Be safe and I'll text you between patients. Love you!"

"I love you too," I said, but the line was dead.

I dropped the phone to my lap and kept watching the snowflakes fall. I knew she wouldn't call for a ride, so I sent Snow a quick text. In a few moments, I got her response. All it said was, *We're on it.*

I smiled and laid the phone on the bed, wheeling from the window to the desk. It was late and I was hungry, but the chances of anything being open or accessible might be slim tonight. I picked up the three-ring binder the hotel provided and flipped it open to the restaurant's page. My eyes traveled the length of them seeing nothing feasible, until something drew my eyes back up the page.

Kiss's Café.

I read the description aloud. "Kiss's Café takes you back to yesteryear when the mashed potatoes were real and the gravy was, too. Our classic dishes are served family-style for large groups. If it's breakfast you want, look no further. We serve your favorite omelets and home fries twenty-four seven. Food so good you might just want to kiss the cook."

I laid the book down on the desk and grabbed my cell phone, typing in the name of the restaurant. There were seven locations in the state and the closest was a block away.

I tapped my phone on my thigh and thought back to the conversation I had with her about the family business. She never told me the name of it, but did say it was a chain. She also didn't mention there were any in Rochester proper.

My eyes drifted back to the window and the falling snow. I shut the phone off and tucked it next to my leg, grabbing my room key. Tonight, I'd have to settle for the pub food in the hotel, but tomorrow morning on my way home, I was going to have to stop and kiss the cook.

Chapter Twelve

By the time I woke up on Saturday morning, the storm had cleared and the sun was shining brightly. I hadn't slept well, tossing and turning a good part of the night from a sore back. I was awakened by my phone ringing a little after nine, nearly vibrating off the nightstand. It was December thanking me for sending Dully over to pick her up after a long night in the ER. Her well-laid plan to sleep most of the night had a monkey wrench thrown in it when a bus accident filled the ER. She assured me the roads were in decent shape now, but she was too tired to drive, so she had accepted the ride from Dully.

She was now safely tucked away at home ready to sleep. I promised to bring Dully over to get her Jeep later and bring it home. It was nice to wake up to her voice, but the voice in my head was screaming at me to ask her about the café. The call ended with me wishing her a good sleep and her wishing me a safe drive, followed by a soft *I love you*. Suddenly, it didn't feel like the right time to bring it up.

After a hot shower, I was never more thankful that my mother insisted I keep a change of clothes and medication in my truck. By the time I was dressed and ready to leave the hotel, it was check-out time and I was hungry.

I drove around the block again looking for a place to park. I had asked for directions when I checked out, but with a grin the clerk had told me, "At the end of the block turn right, you can't miss it." He was right.

The huge lit up pair of scarlet lips on the roof of the building said it all. Obviously, it was a popular place for Saturday morning breakfast. Even at nearly eleven, I couldn't find a place to park. While I waited impatiently for a parking place, I started to question if what I was doing was a good idea. *Getting involved with her family situation might not be the best way to win her over, Jay.*

I drummed my fingers on the hand pedals, my heart pounding at the thought of never seeing her again. Maybe it was the social worker in me, but I felt like I needed to go in and at least see the place where she grew up.

A large group of people came out the door at that moment and separated into five different cars, opening up the perfect spot in front of the door. I slipped my truck into the spot and killed the engine, eyeing the sidewalk. It was scraped down to the bare concrete and there was no ice. Things were looking up. When I left the hotel, I stashed Sport next to me on the seat, since I was going to want to spend as little time in the snow as possible.

"Time to give you a test run on a good old Minnesota winter day," I mumbled.

I set him down on the concrete and slid over into the chair. I locked the truck, talking Sport through the actions I wanted him to take. I was on the sidewalk in less than four commands and incredibly impressed. Score one for Snow. I snickered. Score one for Snow Alexander, I corrected.

I glanced up at the door of the café and scratched my head. It had a small ramp leading into a covered doorway, but no handicapped door opener and not enough room to get the door open without moving the chair all the way back down the ramp. If I got the door open, I'd probably pull my back trying to get in.

I let out a sigh and figured it was a sign to mind my own business. I turned Sport back to my truck, ready to head home.

"Sir, did you want to come in?" a voice asked.

I turned back and noticed a well-dressed man holding the door for me. "Yes, thank you. I just had back surgery and didn't want to hurt myself."

I wheeled through the door and he smiled at me as I passed. I tried to act normal, even though I felt like I'd been punched in the gut. I'd seen that smile before on a certain brown-haired beauty I was in love with.

"I do apologize. I've meant to have the handicapped door opener installed for the last few months. It's sitting in the backroom and I never get to it," he explained, letting the door close. He moved aside a stool from the low counter, so I could pull my chair up and lock it.

I took my gloves off and laid them on the stool next to me. "I'm pretty used to it, but if you have an opener, I would get it installed as quickly as you can. I'd hate to see such a cute little place get fined by the ADA. I've seen it happen before in my hometown."

He nodded, pouring me a cup of coffee before I even asked. He set the pot back down and stuck his hand out. "I'm Noel Kiss, by the way, owner of Kiss's Café."

I shook his hand firmly and raised a brow. "Nice to meet you, Noel. I'm Jay Alexander. I was driving home when the lips caught my attention." I grinned, pointing to the roof.

It was his turn to grin. "Best marketing gimmick ever." His eyes clouded over for a moment at whatever memory had hit him. "The idea came from an old employee. I wonder if she'd remember the conversation."

It took me no time to figure out the old employee was December, so I pulled a menu from between the holder and busied myself looking over it while he stepped away. I wondered if he knew the look he wore on his face when he spoke of her. There was a profound sadness in his voice when he spoke again.

"Anyway, breakfast is on the house to make up for the door fiasco." He motioned at the entry and I glanced up from the menu quickly.

"Oh, it's okay. Really, I understand. It's hard running a business and trying to find time to get everything done."

"No, I insist. What interests you this morning?" he asked, pulling a pad over from across the counter.

I could see I wasn't going to win this battle, so I smiled and laid the menu down on the counter. "In honor of the wonderful winter wonderland we have this morning, I'll have the December Morning omelet with pancakes."

His hand faltered on the pad and he turned away from me, yelling my order into the open window at the cook, who waved as acknowledgment. Noel didn't turn around, instead he rolled silverware into napkins on the counter in front of him. I slipped the menu back in its holder and shrugged out of my coat.

"The manager at the hotel told me this is a chain. Looking around, it doesn't feel like a chain restaurant. It feels like a quaint, family-run, and life invested business," I offered, hoping to engage him again.

He turned and brought the coffee pot back over, refilling my cup. His eyes were trained on a waitress who was chatting at a table where a couple sat with their little boy. The restaurant was otherwise empty now that the breakfast hour was over.

"He was right, technically. We have seven restaurants. This was the first one my father opened before I was even born. Since then, we've grown the café because there are so few places like this anymore. The big chains have taken over the heartland of America, and we want to give families the same kind of dining atmosphere that we grew up with."

"We?" I asked and he nodded.

"My parents started the business and when they passed, I took it over," he explained. I waited for him to mention his sister, but he didn't. "When my mother passed, we had five cafes around Minnesota. When she died, I branded the name and now I try to open one new café a year. I buy the property, and get it up and running while training the store manager for that restaurant here. Once the restaurant is running smoothly, I step back and let the manager take over. My goal is to turn the manager into the owner-operator within three years."

He turned and grabbed two plates from the window, setting them in front of me. The steam from the hot eggs and pancakes warmed my face.

"Wait, you what?" I asked, setting the syrup back down on the counter.

He leaned a hip against the counter. "I don't want to run all these cafes myself, so I go to wherever the new restaurant is and hire the person I think will be most successful at keeping the franchise in the black. We have agreed on terms and when the café is successfully bringing in a certain level of income, anything above and beyond goes into a fund for them to purchase it."

I must have looked confused because he laughed and motioned around the building. "Say the business model says this café should bring in ten grand a month?" he asked and I nodded my understanding. "After a few months, I see that the manager is bringing in thirteen grand or fifteen grand consistently. I take the extra three to five grand and put it in a fund. Within a year they then have the down payment they need to purchase the building and the franchise name. Make sense?" he asked and I nodded again.

"Yeah, that's pretty cool. I've never heard of people doing it that way. Usually, if you want to buy a franchise, you need the money upfront, and lots of it," I said, pouring the hot syrup on my pancakes.

"I don't want to be usual. I want to be honorable. I want Kiss's Café to be known as a family-friendly place in all aspects of its business model, from our customers to our franchise owners and employees. A wise woman once told me *every person you meet in our restaurant has a story. Take the time to listen to it, they just might teach you something.*"

I set my fork down on my plate and chewed slowly, watching the faraway look in his eyes. "Your mother?" I asked and he shook his head.

"No, my sister," he sighed, patted the counter twice, and walked away.

I watched him disappear between the swinging doors into the kitchen area. If he was trying to hide that he missed his sister, he wasn't doing a good job of it.

I cut into my omelet and it melted under the metal fork. My attention turned to the fluffy eggs filled with ham and covered in a white hollandaise sauce that bound all the flavors together, turning it into a beautiful December morning. The only thing that would make it more beautiful would be sharing it with my December. She and her twin shared the same eyes, the same smile, and most likely the same stubborn streak. As I ate, I wondered just exactly what it was that kept them from bridging the gap and having a relationship again. She told me she tried to reach out to him, but he returned her cards and letters unopened.

He came back through the door with filled syrup containers, replacing half-empty ones on the tables around the café. Was it his pride in his business and her need to do something else that was really at the heart of the problem, or was it something more? Twins, even fraternal boy/girl twins, had a special connection, and it must be hard when that was taken away. I could see why December reached out to him, and now I see that it must have broken her heart when he didn't reach back. I wondered what would happen if I brought them together, face-to-face.

I laid my fork down on the counter and sat back in Sport. The omelet was huge and I was stuffed. I was hoping Noel would come back over, but so far he was avoiding me. I was itching to ask him more questions, but knew it was just the social worker in me wanting to fix something that didn't involve me, or maybe wasn't even fixable. It was obvious when he talked about December that he missed her. It was also obvious when December talked about him that she missed him. It made me wonder if the only thing keeping them apart was pure stubbornness.

"How was your breakfast?" Noel asked, finally coming back around the counter.

"Wonderful. That omelet was the best I've ever had. Give my compliments to the cook."

"Hey, Nick, you fooled another one!" he called over his shoulder and the cook hit the bell twice and gave me a thumbs up. Laughter filled the air and the joke was undoubtedly an old one.

I stuck my hand out over the counter and Noel shook it. "Thanks again for breakfast. I'll stop in again, as I'll be in Rochester on and off for business the next few months."

"It was nice meeting you, Jay. Stop by anytime." He grabbed a pamphlet off the rack and handed it to me. "There's a list of our other locations, in case you're ever in their neck of the woods."

"Thanks, you never know where this job will take me," I agreed, sliding it alongside me.

"Where do you work?" he asked, coming around the counter to get the door for me.

"I'm the social worker for Providence Hospital in Snowberry," I answered carefully, watching his face for recognition.

The quick swallow and flash of his eyes told me he knew exactly where his sister lived and worked.

"Great little town." He smiled, but it didn't go all the way to his eyes.

"I like it there, born and raised. Hey, I'll be back down again next Friday. What do you say I stop in on Saturday and install that handicapped door opener for you? It won't take long and I'll bring a friend to help with the stuff up high."

The look of surprise on his face was almost comical. "Really? Do you install door openers on the side or something?"

I shook my head. "No, I've just helped out some of the local businesses at home from time to time. It's really not that hard, and I know how it is when you're busy trying to make a living. It only takes an hour if you know what you're doing. Do you have downtime that I could get it installed without bothering your customers?"

I wasn't going to give him an option to say no to this.

He shrugged. "We're open twenty-four hours a day, so that makes it hard. Our only quiet time on Friday is from about eight to just before the bars close."

I ran December's schedule through my head. She would be off from her twelve-hour shifts on Thursday morning, so a late Friday drive to Rochester shouldn't be a problem. "That's perfect. I'll finish with my business in the evening and we will swing by around nine. Does that work?"

"That would be perfect, but are you sure? You really don't have to. I'm a little embarrassed I didn't make it a priority before now," he admitted.

I waved my hand as he pulled the door open for me. "No worries, I understand. You must be super busy running a business all day every day. I really would hate for you to get fined because someone reports you. The rest of the building meets guidelines and that's more than I can say about a lot of the restaurants in my hometown. Consider it payment for the opportunities you give others through franchising." I wheeled through the door and turned Sport back to face him.

He was smiling when he spoke. "Okay, I'll accept on the condition that you and your friend eat free at any Kiss's Café at any time. I'll make sure my owner-operators know." He stuck his hand out and I shook it.

"It's a deal. See you Friday."

I grinned, turned the chair, and did a mental fist pump on the way to my truck.

Chapter Thirteen

I was just pulling back into town a little after two when my phone rang. I pulled over to the side of the road and answered with my Bluetooth.

"This is Jay," I said quickly, pushing my flashers on.

"Hello, Jay, this is December." She laughed and I smiled.

"I've missed you. I figured you'd be sleeping. Is something wrong?" I asked, worried she was ill.

"Nope, I'm fine. Garrett woke me up and I can't fall back to sleep. I was wondering if you can give me a ride to get my Jeep when you get back to town. I hate to bother Dully again." She sighed. "That's a lie. I just want to see you and I know you can't get into my place."

I chuckled at her admittance. "I want to see you, too. I just pulled into town. Give me five and I'll pick you up at the curb?"

"I'll be waiting," she said then the call ended.

I wore a smile on my face when I pulled back onto the road at the thought of seeing her again. I waited for other parts of me to get excited, too. There were tingles, but there was nothing more. I was trying not to be frustrated by the lack of communication in that department, but the farther out from surgery I was, the more worried I became. If I couldn't perform sexually, how would I be able to have a meaningful relationship with December? *All in good time, Jay*, I reminded myself.

I'd waited a lot of years to be intimate with a woman. Part of it was from fear of rejection or that things wouldn't go smoothly. Part of it was what happened in college. I held onto the hope that when I found the right woman, everything would fall together and she would be accepting of me without expecting more than I could deliver.

The thought of being intimate with December didn't make me nervous or anxious. It just made me fight the need to close my eyes and picture her beautiful body under my hands. Holding her in my arms made my whole day a little sweeter and I knew when we were intimate, it would be the sweetest experience of my life. I'd do everything in my power to make her first time the best, too.

I might not have a lot of experience, but I was well-read and had done my research. I knew what a woman liked and I knew I would probably need some adaptive equipment to help in the future. I wanted her input on that, though. If we were going to be together, then I want her to be part of those decisions. Besides, it will be fun to get to know each other sexually just by exploring what options are available to us.

I did feel a little guilty for what I had plotted

out on the way home, but I reminded myself how much she wants him in her life. She told me about their falling out when their mother died and how in his grief Noel blamed her. I hated that she carried that around with her, feeling guilty for choosing to do something she loved. She was a strong woman with a good head on her shoulders, and she deserved respect from her family. The only family she had left was Noel, and all I could do was pray he was ready to leave the past in the past and start the New Year as a family again.

I turned down her street and saw her standing on the curb, her coat tucked around her, and her feet in a pair of furry boots. She wore a bright blue stocking cap on her head and her hair blew in the breeze from under it. If anyone could be a fashion model for winter wear, it was her. There was a little stirring below the belt area and a smile grew on my face. Maybe things were coming back to life after all. I idled at the curb and reached over, opening the door to the truck. She climbed inside and threw her arms around my neck.

"Hi, I missed you," she whispered.

I hugged her and rubbed her back. "I missed you, too. You look beautiful, but you do look tired."

She leaned back and tucked her hair behind her ears. Her fingers traced the black lines under my eyes. "You don't look too well-rested yourself. Was the hotel uncomfortable?"

"Yeah, I tossed and turned most of the night. I wasn't prepared to stay overnight, but I lived. It wasn't like I was up all night saving lives or any-thing." I winked and she laughed.

I put the car in drive and she put her seatbelt on. "I didn't save any lives, but I did welcome a new one."

I glanced at her from the corner of my eye. "A baby in the emergency room?"

She nodded, a smile wide on her sweet face. "It doesn't happen very often let me tell you, but last night the storm held mom and dad up, so by the time they got to the ER we didn't have time to transfer them. I caught their little baby girl in my arms at three o'clock on the dot. She was just a bit of a thing, and so quiet. She looked around like she was taking the world in."

"You light up when you talk about your work. Do you know that?"

"She was the first baby I've ever delivered. I joked with mom and dad the whole time while everyone ran around getting ready to deliver. Dad was scared, and mom was trying so hard to keep it together. I told them about how my brother and I were born, and our names, then about a doctor in the hospital named Snow. It seemed to calm them and help them focus on doing what needed to be done. I love my job, but being the one to lay that brand-new life in her father's arms still gives me goosebumps. It's probably why I couldn't sleep."

I pulled into my spot in the garage and put it in park, picking up her hand and kissing it. "I'm so proud of you. You always go above and beyond what they ask of you because you care so deeply about people. That's rare these days." I opened my door and grabbed the remote for my chair lift. There was a tug on my coat and I turned to her.

"Why are we in your garage? I thought we were going to pick up my Jeep?"

"We will, later. Right now, we are going to lie down in my bed and rest for a few hours. Then I'll take you to dinner and to get the car."

I turned back to the chair lift and swung it out onto the garage floor, pushing the button to open while she came around and met me at the chair. I slid into it and she grabbed my bag from the bed of the truck, following me down the shoveled path to the house. We held hands and I glanced up at her. "What did they name the baby?"

The smile that lit up her face was captivating. When I looked closer, I noticed her eyes tearing up a little and her chin quivered. "December Noelle."

"Sport, stop," I commanded and swung her onto my lap, right in the middle of the path. "Come here, love," I whispered as she laid her head on my chest. "How incredibly special is that? I'm so proud of you."

She nodded against my shirt and I put Sport in motion and went up the ramp with her on my lap. She was crying softly, and I wasn't sure if it was adrenaline let down or something else.

I got us in the door and helped her take her coat off, letting her settle on the couch. I handed her a tissue discreetly then wheeled to the kitchen and made two cups of hot cocoa, hoping if I avoided coffee, we might get some rest.

I carried the tray back to the living room while Sport drove, and set it on the coffee table. She had herself under better control and sat on the couch with her legs tucked under her. I swung up next to her then handed her a mug.

"Would it be okay if we stop and get a special gift to take the baby when we go pick up your Jeep?" I asked.

"I would love that. I don't know why it wouldn't be okay. You work at the hospital, so we aren't breaking any privacy laws. That would mean a lot to me." She smiled and I rubbed her thigh slowly. Her chin was still quivering a little and I cupped it with my hand.

"Little December Noelle really touched you, didn't she?" I asked and she tried to bite back a sob. "Sweetheart, what am I missing? Is this about Noel?"

She shook her head a little and I took the mug from her hands and then gathered her close. "Tell me what's bothering you. I'm here to listen. I may not be able to fix it, but I'll hold you until you feel better," I promised.

"Today is December eighth." She fisted my shirt sleeve in her fingers and sobbed a little against my chest. "I was holding a brand-new baby girl on the anniversary of my mother's death, which was also the day I lost my brother, forever."

I rocked her back and forth gently, kissing the

top of her head and rubbing her back. I didn't see that coming. I thought back to my early meeting at the restaurant and suddenly all the pieces fell together and it all made sense. "How many years, honey?"

"Eight. She died just a few days after our eighteenth birthday, just a few hours after I told her I was going to college for nursing and not working in the family business. I told her that's what daddy wanted for me, too. She refused to believe me. She was angry and screamed that I didn't care about the life she and Dad had given me. If I truly loved them, I wouldn't run away. I tried to tell her that Daddy wanted me to do what I loved, and that the business wasn't making him happy either. She stormed out and I never saw her alive again."

"I'm sorry, December. I'm so sorry," I whispered, letting her lay against me and soak up whatever it was she needed from me. "I love you, sweetheart, and I know deep down your mom did, too. She was just upset and scared. No one blames you for what happened."

"Noel does," she whispered. "The last time I saw him it ended in him screaming at me that I'm the reason she's dead and if he never sees me again it would be too soon. I sat in the back of the church at her funeral and all other communication was done through lawyers. I lost so much by choosing to do what I love. Why does it have to be like this? I wish nothing but happiness for Noel. Why does he think I don't deserve the same?"

I held her to me and kissed her cheek. "He was hurting, and when people are grieving, they don't always behave rationally. You've gone through a lot in your short life, and I think you're one of the strongest people I know. Losing one parent is hard, but losing both in your teens is something I can't even wrap my mind around."

She shrugged a little, her body tired from the hours of work and the fatigue that only crying can bring. "Mom wasn't going to live long. She died of a massive aortic artery dissection. Whether she had argued with me or had gone to work and picked up something a little too heavy, she was going to die. I know that in my head, but in my heart, I feel like the catalyst that destroyed our family."

"You're not," I whispered, trying to soothe her. "You don't deserve what happened. I wish you could talk to Noel and work toward being part of a family again."

She sat up and wiped her face just as the doorbell rang. "I'll get it." I patted her leg and scooted into the chair, certain I knew who the visitor was. I opened the door and Sunny stood on the doorstep, holding a bowl in front of her.

"Hi, baby girl. I've missed you!" I sang, letting her in the door. She grinned at me and held out the bowl. I took it and set it on the coffee table while she closed the door.

"Mommy made your favorite beef stew and asked me to bring it to you. She said you might be hungry. Hello, Miss December." She waved shyly at

December sitting on the couch.

December smiled and waved back. "Hi, Sunny, it's nice to see you again. Have you been making snowmen in all this new snow?"

Sunny walked over to her slowly and climbed up on the couch next to her. "Why are you sad? Was my little Jaybird bad?"

I tried not to laugh, and December chuckled, patting Sunny's hand. "No, sweetheart, Jay didn't do anything bad. He was giving me a hug to make me feel better. I'm sad today because I miss my mom, but I'll be okay," she promised, squeezing Sunny's hand.

"Why don't you just call your mom if you miss her? I'm sure she wouldn't want you to be sad," Sunny questioned.

I rolled the chair over to the couch, ready to grab her and distract her, but December just smiled at her.

"I'd love to do that, Sunny, but my mom is in heaven. I can't call her."

Sunny nodded her head. "Yes, you can. You can call her. Just do this." She took December's hands and folded them together. "Now you just say, Mom, are you there? It's me, December. She will answer if you do that, I promise."

I could see December was near tears again and as sweet as this little girl was, I needed to rescue her. I picked Sun up and set her on my lap, whispering in her ear. She looked at me with big eyes and nodded her head solemnly.

She climbed down off my chair and hugged December around the waist. "I'll see you again real soon, Miss December. I gotta go home and help daddy with his lessons."

December didn't speak, but hugged her back and nodded her head at her words. I took Sunny's hand and helped her to the door, then kissed her cheek.

"Will you tell Mommy and Daddy that we're going to rest for a little while and then will be leaving again? Oh, and make sure your mommy knows I said thank you for the stew." I rubbed my belly and licked my lips while she giggled at my silliness.

"I'll tell them. Can I watch the game with you tomorrow? I miss you," she said, her face falling a little.

I gave her a high five and then a tickle. "I miss you, too. Of course, we can watch the game tomorrow. I'll be up by kick-off time if not sooner, okay?"

She nodded happily and skipped down the deck and up the path. I pushed the door closed and spun back around to see December putting the stew in the fridge. She was exhausted and her shoulders were slumped. She turned back around to me and I held my hand out. "She's an old soul, too."

I smiled and she took my hand.

"She is. I love her already. She's not like most little ones. She's very observant and empathetic. Most kids her age can't think about anyone but themselves."

I wheeled down to my bedroom, letting her in the door first. "You're right, but Sunny isn't like most kids. She's grown up with a mother and an uncle in wheelchairs. Being in a home like that changes your perspective on your independence, your selfishness, and your own abilities. Sunny has always been able to pick up on someone hurting, physically or emotionally. I think that's why she's always been my shadow. She knew from the second they laid her in my arms that I needed her."

She knelt in front of my chair and kissed me, her lips cold against mine. I held her face in my hands and kissed her until they warmed, melting against mine. I slowed the kiss and pulled away, not wanting to break the connection she yearned for, but knowing she was tired and needed sleep.

"Let's rest for a few hours. You're exhausted and my back is sore. I need to use the bathroom and then we can stretch out." I backed the chair toward the bathroom door and she nodded.

I turned Sport and went into the bathroom, closing the door behind me and sighing. In one week, I had a chance to bring these two people back together again. Two people who have been hurting for the same reason, but unable to bridge the void between them. I was going to have to be that bridge, and I was going to have to get it exactly right the first time.

"Can I help you find something?" Dully asked and I wheeled my chair away from the cupboard.

"Yeah, Sunny wants those graham cracker bear things. Where are they?" I asked exasperated.

"You mean Teddy Grahams? We're out." He grinned and I hung my head.

"Better think of a replacement. The Vikings are down by seven and she's not a happy camper."

He grabbed something out of the cupboard and poured some in a bowl. "I'll take these to her. It's half time and this will appease the angry God of football. Stay here, I want to talk to you."

He disappeared around the corner and I groaned. Wonder what he wanted to talk about now. I grabbed a beer from the fridge and popped off the cap, taking a swig of the white Belgian brew. Yesterday afternoon, after napping, I took December shopping for a baby gift at Savannah's, and then to the hospital to meet Ember, which is apparently the nickname of the barely twelve-hour old beauty who was her namesake. We had decided to stop into Savannah's shop to get flowers for her mom, Joni, and we were glad we did. She had a beautiful handmade baby afghan and layette set that was perfect for the occasion.

I sat and watched December holding Ember and prayed someday she'd be holding ours. It seemed so sudden to be thinking those kinds of thoughts, but I was. I'd known December barely a month, but it was like she's been part of my life forever. We had an easy-going, loving rapport with each other, which was wonderful. When we left the hospital, she met me in her Jeep at Gallo's for some beer and pizza. I hated having to let her go last night, but she needed to sleep before work today. She was still sad about her mom, but at least she was smiling by the time she left the restaurant. Something told me when she got to work today, she'd be back up on the maternity ward with a certain little girl in her arms.

"She wasn't too pleased she had to settle for Scooby-Doo bones, but I snuck her a root beer and that did the trick," Dully said, coming back into the kitchen.

"She's a little spitfire. How did you sneak a root beer with Snow sitting right there?" I asked, setting my bottle on the table.

"Easy. Snow was fed up with her crankiness over football while she was trying to work, so she motioned her eyes toward the sodas. I grabbed one and gave it to Sunny, and now both of my girls are happy." He bowed and I laughed, shaking my head at the mental image I had.

Dully grabbed a beer and sat down at the table, cracking it open. "Sunny told me December was at your place again yesterday."

I nodded. "She was having a hard day, so I was trying to be a good friend."

He raised a brow in response. "Sunny said December was crying when she got there and was sad about her mommy in heaven."

I twirled the beer bottle on the table. "Yup, she

reported correctly. Yesterday was the anniversary of her mom's death, and she was struggling. She has a twin brother she never sees, and he's all she has left for a family."

Dully set his bottle down. "A twin brother? I had no idea. Does he live far away?"

"Nope. He lives in Rochester. I met him yesterday," I admitted and he cleared his throat.

"What? Why don't they see each other if he's only an hour away?"

"Her brother blames December for their mother's death. She didn't want to work in the family restaurants, and shortly after she told her mother she was going to nursing school, her mother died of an aortic dissection. It wasn't December's fault, of course, but you know how people sometimes need someone to blame."

Dully nodded thoughtfully. "I do, but what I don't understand is how you met him."

I sighed heavily. "I stopped at the restaurant yesterday on the way home. I didn't expect to meet him. I just wanted to see the place where she grew up. He was there and we struck up a conversation. I didn't let on that I knew December, but he talked about her a lot, and I think he misses her, too."

"You really like this girl, don't you, Jay?" he asked, surprised.

I shook my head. "No, I love her. I love her the way you love Snow, unconditionally and with a fever pitch I didn't know existed within me."

Dully sat back and smiled. "Well, here I

thought I was going to have a whole discussion about love with you. We can all see how much you love her, and we wondered how you were feeling. Does December know?"

"I told her on her birthday. I didn't mean to, but it slipped out. I told her she didn't have to say it back, but I wanted her to know how I felt. I was giving her a chance to walk away if she needed to." I motioned at the chair and rolled my eyes a little.

"Instead, she came to your bed," Dully said.

"No, it wasn't like that!" I exclaimed and his hand shot forward.

"Jay, sorry, I just meant she came to you when she needed you. I wasn't prying into your personal life. I apologize, that was a poor choice of words."

I swallowed back my anxiety and took a breath. "It's okay, you know how I get about that. I'm trying to do everything right. She's really wonderful, but it hasn't gone that far. Things still aren't working great in that department, but it is improving."

"She understands your limitations?" Dully asked and I nodded.

"I was upfront about everything. I had to be, considering how things are right now," I admitted.

"What did she say?" he asked and I scrunched my eye a little. He held up his hands in deference to the question. "Sorry, forget I asked. You obviously worked it out."

"She said the same thing you did, that I need to give it time after the surgery. She said if we decide to become intimate and I need help, she'll go with me to the clinic to get it."

Dully's eyebrows went almost to his hairline. "Really? I wasn't expecting that."

"Me either, but she said if we were ready to be intimate, then we were ready to share everything, at least as far as she was concerned. She's an amazing woman with a good heart. I think she will fit in nicely with our family." I smiled and he nodded.

"She is. Mom and Dad love her already. I drove her home yesterday from the hospital and she wouldn't stop thanking us for coming out. We think she's pretty great, and she has Sunny's seal of approval, so you have our blessing."

"Sunny's seal of approval, huh? That's big stuff right there. She's a good judge of character." I laughed and so did Dully.

"She's a ballbuster is what she is. She kept looking for excuses to come down there and check her out the first time you brought her home. She came back up the path and told us, "My little Jaybird is wearing a smile and Miss December is beautiful. She can stay.""

I snorted while drinking and beer came out my nose. I swiped at my face while half-laughing, half-choking. "I love her. She does make me laugh. Did she tell you we texted for an hour when I was in Rochester using nothing but emojis? She's a smart one. You're going to have your hands full, my brother."

"Tell me about it. Snow is talking about another little one soon, but we might need to conserve our energy for her teenage years. Hey, I never did find out why you were in Rochester. Did the hospital send you over?" he asked and I wondered why Snow hadn't told him.

"Another little one, you say? I wouldn't object, but you're right, better up your game 'cause you could end up with another one of her." I laughed and he did, too. I was quiet, though, in case the girls were listening. "As far as Rochester, I was there on hospital business. They asked me to pick up and run with the fundraising calendar the hospital does every year. We're really running late on it since January is just around the corner. I needed to come up with something uncomplicated yet sellable, so I was in Rochester seeing a friend of mine. He does model photography and offered to do the shoot free of charge. If I can find a printer who's willing to print them for cost, then we'll be all set, and I can still get them out by the first of the year."

Dully set his beer down. "So, what's it going to be this year?"

"This year's calendar is going to be a modeling photo shoot with kids from the community with neuro-spinal conditions like spina bifida and paralysis. It will be shots of them doing everyday things from their chairs, kind of like I used to do when I modeled," I explained and he was nodding along.

"That's never been done before. What a great idea! Imagine how much fun those kids are going to have. I'm guessing Rochester is going to be a bit of a drive for a lot of the kids, though," he said slowly.

"Noble will come to Snowberry. He understands the kids have travel limitations, and he doesn't have a studio anyway. We'll take photos in different places throughout the community. I might need your help because I was thinking I'd love a shot of all the kids together for the cover of the calendar. We may need to use the school."

Dully gave me a thumbs up. "I can absolutely help with that. Is the money going to go to the children's foundation then?"

I shook my head. "No, it's pending board approval right now, but we're hoping they will approve our idea. I've requested a fund be set up and held until spring when we can build Sunnytime Playground."

"Sunnytime playground?" he asked perplexed and I chuckled.

"Yes, Sunnytime Playground, Snowberry's first barrier-free playground, Dully. It'll be built at the school because it's also a city park. It'll be a place where all the kids can play regardless of their limitations, and where Snow can take Sunny and finally be able to interact with her."

Dully had a huge smile on his face. "Sunnytime Playground, I get it now. You know I've been lobbying with the PTA to build a barrier-free playground for years. The cost is astronomical, and we haven't been able to raise the funds. We have about ten thousand raised and another twenty-five thousand in a grant we just got a few weeks ago. We need about another twenty-five thousand to make it a reality. I can't believe this. Did Snow tell you about the playground?"

I shook my head in surprise. "I honestly had no idea you were working with the PTA on this, brother. It was purely a selfish idea because I remember what it was like not being able to play on the playground at recess. It's time that everyone in the community has someplace safe and fun to play. Knowing you have that much money ready to go tells me this will be a reality come spring." I grinned and he reached over, giving me a high five.

"I knew keeping you around here was going be a good thing, little brother. Let's tell Snow she will finally have a place to take Sunny." He leaned back to yell, but I stopped him.

"She knows, Dully, she's on the board. I'm a little surprised she didn't tell you," I admitted and he turned back to me.

"Oh, yeah. Hmmm, me too, actually. She knows I've been working on this for years."

"I didn't tell you because it was Jay's idea, and he deserved to be the one to finally make your dream a reality." Snow said, coming up behind her husband. She looped her arms around his neck from behind and leaned her chin on the back of his chair. "And, the board has approved Sunnytime Playground as the recipient of the funds this year. I filled them in on the fundraising efforts in the community already, so they were thrilled to be on board with it. They will deposit the funds into the account you already have set up with the bank."

Dully reached up and hugged her arms, "You two rock, you know that? The kids in this community deserve a place like this. I spend so much time at recess trying to keep our kids happy and distracted while the other kids get to play. They will finally feel included for the first time in their lives."

Snow patted his chest. "They do deserve this and word is spreading among the board members. We already have all the backfill we'll need to get the ground ready, and a group of construction guys willing to donate their time."

"That's great, Snow. How much fun would it be to break ground as soon as spring arrives? I can't wait to take Sunny to Sunnytime playground." I laughed and she raised a brow.

"And maybe someday, a little one of your own?" she asked and I sighed.

"From your lips to God's ear." I blew her a kiss and she winked at me before turning and rolling from the room.

KISS

I tossed my pen onto my desk and set my head in my hands. It was Thursday and I was exhausted. I spent the afternoon and evening yesterday keeping everything organized for the calendar photoshoot. The whole thing had gone off without a hitch, but by the time my head hit the pillow, it was well after midnight. Now, it was barely one in the afternoon and I was ready for bed. It might be that my brain was guilting me into exhaustion, though.

Yesterday had been so much fun, and December had come along to help. We spent the entire day together, and I never once mentioned my plans to take her to see her brother tomorrow night. She agreed to go with me to Rochester to pick up the proofs from the photoshoot, but I omitted the rest of the plans for the evening.

I picked up a couple of Tums and started chewing them, guilt lacing the action. I deserved the heartburn I was suffering from.

She was so sweet and loving to the kids yesterday it made my heart ache. People say it's important to teach children empathy, but some people you don't have to teach. Some people just exude it, and December is one of those people. Yesterday, when one of the little ones got upset because his wheelchair stopped working, she carried him around on her back while they fixed his chair. She never gave it a second thought, but Jon had a huge grin on his face the entire day.

A smile tipped my own lips just as my phone rang. "This is Jay Alexander," I answered.

"Jay, it's December. Listen, there's a problem," she said quietly. She sounded out of breath and scared.

"What's the problem? How can I help?" I asked, trying to keep her calm.

"Can you come to the ER? It's Snow. Snow's in the ER and she's really sick. I think you should come down here," she said again, her voice laced with concern.

"Sport, forward, basketball," I said, rolling out the door with my cell phone at my ear. "I'm coming down, sweetheart. Did you call Dully?"

"No, I don't have his number. I have to look it up. She came down without her phone and she can't tell me the number," she said flustered.

"December, I'll call him. Will they let you stay with Snow? Was she in an accident?" I asked, pushing the elevator button repeatedly.

"No, no, she just got really sick in a meeting and passed out. She hit her head on the table and now she's vomiting. I have to go," she said quickly and the line went dead.

I rolled the chair into the elevator with the cell phone tucked under my ear, frantically pushing the button for the ground floor and begging for cell phone service in the elevator. All I could do was hope he had his phone on him and wasn't teaching. I didn't have time to go through the school secretary.

The ride down took forever while the phone rang in my ear. When it picked up, I heard static and then Dully's voice. "Snow's in trouble, I'm on my way there!" he shouted into the phone.

"Dully, slow down and be careful. I'm almost to the ER. December didn't think anyone had called you." I went for calm, but his anxiety was ramping mine up, too.

"Liam called when he heard what happened. I'll be there in ten minutes. God, she has to be all right," he whispered so quietly I barely heard him over the sound of the tires on the pavement.

"She's going to be okay, Dully. Drive carefully, so you don't need a bed next to her. I'll keep you updated. I'm hanging up now." I pushed the off button and the chair was already rolling before the door was even open.

I caught the first person in scrubs and grabbed their shirt. "Where's Snow Alexander?"

The guy pointed to the third curtain and I wheeled my chair closer, not wanting to go behind the curtain since there were several sets of feet around the stretcher.

"Jay!" I turned, and December was jogging toward me from another cubicle.

"How is she?" I asked without preamble and she took my hand, kneeling next to the chair to whisper in my ear.

"She's okay. She came to and has a slight concussion. We finally got her vomiting under control with some antiemetics and fluids. She's with the doctors now. Did you get Dully?" she whisper-asked and I nodded.

"He's on his way here. It shouldn't take him but five minutes as frantic as he was. He's freaking out. Liam called him and said she was sick," I explained, my own breathing ragged. "How did she hit her head when she was in her chair?"

"From what they told us, she wasn't in her chair. She was sitting in a boardroom chair while someone else was doing a demonstration with MAC. All I know is, she got really sick and before anyone could move, she passed out. She hit her head on the side of the table and collapsed to the floor. They think she might have a broken wrist," she explained hurriedly, but she looked sick herself just relating what happened. "I have to go back to my other patient. When Dully gets here, steer him to the lounge until the doc comes for him. They shouldn't be much longer."

I took her hand and held it to my cheek for a second. "Thank you for being here. I'll go intercept him at the doors. Keep us posted if anything changes."

She nodded and hurried back to the other curtain. I wheeled out toward the waiting room, trying to put my social worker face on instead of my scared to death brother-in-law face. I was going to need it if I was going to keep Dully out of the ER. I watched him run full speed at the doors, barely waiting for them to open before squeezing through. He came barreling into the room, his hair wild from the trip across the parking lot.

"Dully," I said, my voice restrained but firm. His eyes were scary crazy when he ran over to me, grabbing my shirt.

"Where is she?" he asked frantically, and I had to grab his forearms and hold him still.

"She's with the doctors. I've talked to the nurse.

They want us to wait in the family room until they come to get us."

He shook his head. "No, I want to see her. You can't keep me from seeing her."

As much as I hated to admit it, he was right, but I had to try. I kept a firm hold on his arms and fought against the pressure of his hand on my chest. "Dully, the doctors really need to make sure she's feeling okay and you can't be in the way. Take a deep breath and think for a minute," I ordered, his eyes finally meeting mine head-on. There was so much fear in them I had to swallow back my own.

Without more words spoken, I guided him to the small family room and he fell into a chair. He ran his hands over his face and his hands trembled. "Tell me what happened."

"December said Snow was in a meeting and sitting in a regular chair because someone was using MAC for a demonstration. She suddenly got sick, and before anyone could get to her, she passed out and hit her head on the way down, falling out of the chair. When she woke up down here, she started vomiting, but they have that under control. Doctors are with her now checking for a broken wrist."

"God, I knew something was wrong this morning, but she wouldn't listen to me," he groaned, rubbing his thighs to keep his hands busy.

"Was she sick this morning, too?" I asked, surprised he let her go to work.

"No, not physically anyway, but she didn't look well. She hasn't looked well for a couple of days. She hasn't been eating much and has spent a lot more time in bed. I just figured she picked up a little bug at the hospital or from Sunny. I should have made her stay home."

I laughed hysterically for a moment. "Like you're going to stop that little thing from doing anything she wants to do."

He pinned me with a big brother look. "I do have some tricks up my sleeve. I should have pulled the plug."

"She wouldn't have listened to you if you had pulled the plug. She still would have gone to work," I insisted.

"When I say pull the plug, I mean the plug on MAC. If I take out the main USB card, she's not going anywhere." He grinned and I just shook my head at him.

"Okay, you win on that one." I checked my watch. It had been about twenty minutes since I'd talked to December and I was getting worried again. It shouldn't take this long to get an x-ray on the arm. "Let me go check with December and see what she knows."

"I'll come with you," he said, standing, but I pointed at the chair.

"No, stay here. They may not be..." I looked up when I saw movement at the door and a nurse stood there waiting.

"Mr. Alexander?" she asked.

"Yes." We both answered in unison and all three of us couldn't hide our smiles.

"Sorry, I'm looking for Snow's husband," she clarified and Dully moved to the door.

"That's me. Is she okay?" he asked her worriedly and she nodded.

"She's going to be fine. The doctor would like me to bring you back now."

Dully nodded and followed her out. I trailed behind and waited by the nurse's station when he stepped behind the curtain. I could only see two sets of feet, one on each side of the bed. There was nothing but murmuring and I was getting frustrated with the amount of time it was taking. The curtain was finally pulled aside and the doctor left with a smile on his face. The curtain fell closed again before I could make eye contact with Dully.

December held up a finger to me and slipped behind the curtain for a few minutes, then pulled it aside and motioned me in. I rolled Sport forward and was relieved to see the smile on December's face. She wouldn't be smiling if Snow was really in danger. She let the curtain fall behind my chair and I went to the other side of the bed opposite Dully. He was in a chair holding her hand and stroking her forehead that was now sporting a large bruise.

The arm closest to me was in a plaster cast, so I laid my arm on the bed and touched her fingers. "You scared us, little lady."

December's hand sat on my shoulder and I appreciated her comfort, even if everything was going to be okay.

Snow rolled her head carefully toward me and offered a smile. "I'm sorry I worried everyone. I didn't feel like eating this morning before I went to the meeting. I started getting overheated and then agitated because they had my chair and I couldn't leave the room. I don't remember much after that. Thanks for keeping Dully calm while you waited."

I smiled and winked. "It was my pleasure. For once, little brother got to tell big brother what to do."

She snickered a little and gave me a fake fist pump with her casted arm the best she could.

"Sunny's going to love that cast. She's going to doodle on it all day long," I teased and she pulled it up to look at it, almost as if she had forgotten it was there.

Her brow furrowed. "Sunny! We have to get Sunny and tell her!" she exclaimed, trying to sit up, but Dully held her to the bed carefully.

"Snow, she's at school. She thinks everything is fine and we aren't going to worry her. I'll take you home and then go pick her up just like always. I want her to be home before she finds out, in case she gets upset," Dully explained logically.

Snow settled a little back against the pillows and rolled her head toward her husband. "Do you think she's going to be upset? She's so loving and sweet. I think she's going to be happy."

Her eyes went closed for a moment and I glanced at Dully. "Do they need to keep her overnight? Why would Sunny be happy she's hurt. I think they should observe her for the night." I turned and stared at December, but her face was neutral.

Snow opened her eyes and took a piece of paper from Dully, handing it over to me. "She's going to be frantic when she finds out I broke my arm, but I'll show her that, and then she'll be happy," she whispered.

I gazed down at the sheet of paper in my hand for the longest time. The images on the paper were jumping out at me, almost in 3D. I looked up again at the two of them, my mouth open. "But, but," I stuttered and Dully laughed as if he couldn't believe it, either.

"But what? Aren't you going to congratulate us? Or maybe we should congratulate you. Congratulations, you're going to be Uncle Jay all over again in May." Dully grinned, reaching across the bed and squeezing my shoulder.

I glanced down at the pictures and then laid my hand on Snow's tummy since I couldn't stand and hug her. She put her hand over mine and patted it.

"I can't believe this. May? Did you know you were pregnant?" I asked, stunned.

They both shook their heads in unison, but Snow spoke. "We had no idea. The doctors think I'm about sixteen weeks already. They did a quick ultrasound today to make sure everything was okay. It is, so I'll go see Dr. Montag next week for a longer scan and appointment," she gushed with happiness.

I put my hand over my mouth and tried to keep it from shaking, but Dully looked up at December and back to me. She squatted next to me and did that thing nurses do. "Jay, are you okay? Do I need to call for a doctor?"

I shook my head, locking eyes with her. "She's already sixteen weeks. This isn't good. She didn't know, just like my mom didn't know with me."

"Okay, Jay, you need to stay calm. This happens quite often to women. The doctors will make sure she's taken care of," December promised, a soothing hand on my arm.

"It's too late already. If there's something wrong, it's too late to prevent it," I whispered, shock filling my voice.

I looked back to Snow, who motioned for Dully to help her sit up. He put a supporting arm behind her back and she took my hand, looking me straight in the eye. "I know you're worried, Jay, but you can't do this to yourself or the family. Your mom took folic acid when she was pregnant with you. It wasn't her fault that you had a neural tube defect. It just happens sometimes. Folic acid can lower the chances, but if it's going to happen, it's going to happen. I take folic acid every day for my bones, so that precaution was taken. I know you're worried, but the doctors said the ultrasound looked good as far as the spine was concerned. It's a little early yet, but they assured me they would do the more in-depth scan in a few weeks and that would tell us for sure. You know spina bifida isn't hereditary, so this baby is at no greater risk than Sunny was. I want you to calm down and think about Sunny. Picture her little face when she finds out she's going to be a big sister, and, it might be another girl!"

I held her good hand carefully and nodded as she spoke, letting her words sink in and lower my heart rate. "You're right, I know you're right. I guess I just get worried because this wasn't planned. I knew you were thinking about it, but I'm sorry. I just, man, I'm so surprised right now." I kissed her hand gently and laid it back down. "I'm so happy for you both and for Sunny. You're such good parents and she's going to be a great big sister, especially to a little sister." I breathed a sigh of relief and tried to relax the tension in my back. "Wait, can they tell it's a girl already?"

Snow gave me a little wink. "Believe me, we were just as surprised, but we're very happy." She gazed up at Dully, who was smiling tenderly at her.

He nodded in agreement. "I'm in a little bit of shock, too. I went from so much fear to so much happiness in a span of a few minutes. Especially when they told me it might be a girl. They said they can't confirm it yet, so we won't say anything to Sunny until we know for sure."

A grin filled my face and I nodded. "Mums the word, but oh, how I can't wait to see her sweet little face when her dream of being a big sister comes true."

Chapter Fourteen

December reached out and turned down the volume on the radio. "You've been sitting there smiling for the last ten miles. What are you thinking about?"

I glanced at her from the corner of my eye. She was smiling brightly and had finally taken her hat off and laid it on the seat.

"I was just thinking about Wednesday and how fun that photoshoot was. I've done a lot of photoshoots in my life, but that is one I'll never forget."

"I'm so glad you invited me to help. I never would have met those amazing kids otherwise. Someday, I'd like to adopt a special needs child. They really steal your heart."

My head swiveled her direction quickly for a second, "Really?"

I looked back to the road but caught her nod. "Yeah, really. Do you want kids, Jay?"

"Yes, I do. I always have. I come from a big family and I want that same kind of life. Do you want kids?" I asked. "I mean, kids of your own."

"I can't wait to be a mother. It's the only other thing I've dreamed about besides being a nurse.

Being a mommy will be the best job ever. I have to admit, I have baby fever after spending the night with Ember Wednesday, and now Snow! I'm still reeling from that one." She laughed and I blew her a kiss since I couldn't take my hands off the controls.

"That was so nice of Joni and Dan to let Ember be in the shoot. Most new moms and dads would never let their newborn be in the hands of a ten-year-old in a wheelchair, but they didn't blink an eye. I think Ember will have a forever friend in Sadie. Did you see how their eyes connected in those shots? It was like they were one soul. Noble really has a great eye."

Sadie also has spina bifida and decided she wanted to portray being a caregiver. It was December's idea to ask Joni, and I'll admit I had doubted they'd agree. She was right and I had a feeling Sadie and Ember would steal the show.

"The community is supportive of everything the hospital does. I think it just comes naturally to them to be helpful. So many of those photos made me cry, but in a good way."

"They were amazing, are ya kidding me with this?" I asked in the worst Brooklyn accent ever.

She snickered, which was to hide the tears still in her eyes since we'd left Noble's. "You bring that mock-up calendar back next week to the board and the moment you leave, they're going to pat themselves on the back for hiring you. You've hit a home run straight out of the gate. I'm proud of you. I love you, Jay."

I gave her an appreciative smile. "I love you too, and thank you. I am a little nervous about pulling all this off, but after seeing those photos, I know we've got this."

"We?" she asked and I nodded.

"Yeah, we. Us. You and me. The community. Whoever you want *we* to be." I sounded like an idiot and needed to change the subject quickly. "Would you really consider adopting a special needs child? That can be pretty intense. I can remember every single one of my surgeries over the years, and if I counted them all, I wouldn't have any fingers left over. That's a lot to sign up for." I shrugged a little, trying to get my head in the right game. Now that the meeting with Noble was over, I had to get gas and then head to the café.

"I know, but I want to be a mommy, and I'm also a nurse. There are kids out there that don't have either and need both."

I turned into a Mobil station and pulled up to a pump, finally putting the truck in park. I turned to her and picked up her hand. "I love your heart. It's so kind and honest. Don't ever change."

She reached up and ran her thumb across my lips. "I could say the same for you," she whispered, leaning in for a kiss. I swallowed hard, knowing I wasn't being so honest right now. I was tricking her into a situation that she wasn't going to be comfortable going into. Doubt crept in as I gazed into her eyes, and I started second-guessing myself. She noticed I didn't return the kiss and leaned back. "Are you okay?"

I motioned out to the pump. "Yeah, I'm okay, just..."

She turned and snickered a little at the old lady watching us.

She cracked open the door and hopped out like nothing happened. "Want me to fill it up?" she asked and I unbuckled my belt.

"I can do it. Get back in here where it's warm," I said, grabbing the remote for the chair lift.

She leaned back in the door and held my eye. "Jason Alexander, I am more than capable of putting gas in a tank. It doesn't make sense for you to get the chair out when I'm standing right here. If we're going to be in a relationship together, you're going to have to agree to some common sense rules. The first rule is if I can do something, and I want to do said thing, then you should let me do it, okay?"

I started to laugh at her with her cheeks sucked in and her eyes on fire. In my defense, the old woman was snickering, too. We both heard her say, "You tell him, honey!"

December lost her battle with the giggles and started to laugh. I leaned over and kissed her smack on the lips. "The only part I heard in all of that was *in a relationship together*, so as far as I'm concerned, whatever else you said is a yes from me. Fill it up," I whispered.

She backed out of the door and shut it, while

I rolled the window down so we could talk. She leaned against the door and gazed out over the highway. "It's eight o'clock now. Do you want to drive back to Snowberry and grab a bite to eat?"

I probably looked like the proverbial deer in the headlights at her question. "I kind of have to go help a friend install a handicapped door opener at his restaurant. I'll need some help at the top of the door, so I was hoping you'd help? Dinner's on him then."

"You're installing handicapped door openers now?" The look she gave me was quizzical, but she was smiling.

"I do it now and again with Dully. For a good long while, most of Snowberry wasn't handicapped accessible. We would have the owners buy the unit and then we'd install it for them free of charge. It was my Eagle Scout project in my senior year of high school," I explained.

"I didn't know you were an Eagle Scout, that's cool, Jay. I bet the owners appreciated having someone who could help install them. Here's the problem, I don't have a clue what I'm doing."

I winked at her nonchalantly, even though I was nervous as hell. "That's okay, mostly it's just holding it and tightening a few bolts. He said the restaurant is quiet between nine and bar closing, so he, or his cook, can help if we get in a pinch."

"Okay, I'm in. What's this place called?" she asked and I swallowed, averting my eyes.

"Kiss's Café." My voice squeaked, but all I heard

was her sharp intake of breath.

She took a step back, her whole body shaking and nearly tripped backward over the pump island. She righted herself and turned, running towards the side of the building.

"December!" I yelled, needing her to stop, but knowing she wouldn't. I leaned my head back on the seat and banged it a little. "Stupid idea, Jay. What in the heck did you think was going to happen?" I asked the empty air.

I was totally helpless to chase her and felt my impotence all the way to my soul. The gas pump clicked off, dragging me back to reality. I pushed the door open, grabbed the lift remote and got my chair down on the ground. I waited impatiently while it opened and then transferred into it, wheeling behind the truck. I unhooked the nozzle and slammed it into the pump, screwed the cap back on, and slapped the fuel door closed.

I rolled into the small station and threw some cash on the counter. "Do you have a restroom?"

The guy eyed me up and nodded, pointing out the door. "Around the side, man. No key needed. If the door is open, it ain't occupied."

He handed me my change and I thanked him, pushing the door open and following the sidewalk around the side of the station. I was pleasantly surprised that it was handicapped accessible. The bathrooms sat next to each other and the men's room was unoccupied. The woman's bathroom was locked tight when I jiggled the handle.

"December, come out, honey," I begged, but there was silence within. "I know you're in there, sweetheart. I'm sorry I upset you. Let me take you home."

I leaned my ear against the door and heard soft sobbing on the other side. I was going to throw up. I was so angry with myself for not being straight with her when I had plenty of opportunities to be.

"I understand that you're upset with me, December, but you have to let me get you home safely. After that, you never have to talk to me again. Just come out so I can make sure you're okay."

The door handle turned and I backed up out of the way. She stepped through the door onto the sidewalk and her face was wet with tears. "Why, Jay?" she whispered so softly I almost didn't hear the question. She had her arms wrapped around herself and she shivered in the cold night.

I held my hand out tentatively. "Come back to the truck, you don't even have your coat. I'll explain once you're somewhere warm."

She didn't move or reach for my hand, almost as if she was in a trance. I rolled as close as I could and took her hand. She didn't pull away, but she didn't squeeze my hand back. "Sport forward hands," I said and led her down the sidewalk, helping her into the truck. I shut the door and rolled around, hoisting myself into the truck and stowing my chair in the back. I turned the heat up on high and moved the truck a short distance away from the pumps.

She leaned against the door and stared at her feet. I was never more grateful for not having a gear-shifter on the floor than I was at this moment. I scooted closer to her and tried to pull her to me, but she resisted. I expected anger, but that wasn't the vibe she gave off. Instead, overwhelming sadness filled her. I eased back a bit but kept my arm around her waist. "I didn't plan this, December. If that's what you think."

"How could you not plan it? You had to have known it was my brother when he introduced himself!" she exclaimed.

"What I mean is, yes, I went to the café last weekend knowing it was your family's restaurant. I didn't go to stick my nose in your relationship with your brother. I went there to see the place where you grew up. I wanted to see the place where you learned to be the wonderful, sweet, and smart woman that you are. I never expected him to be there. I just wanted to understand where you were coming from a little bit better."

"And now you're such good buddies with my brother that you're installing a door opener for him?" she asked skeptically. "Sorry if I find that hard to believe."

I sighed with resignation. "I know this looks bad, but it's true. I got to the restaurant and couldn't open the door to get in. A guy opened the door for me and apologized for not having a handicapped door opener. His smile was one I'd seen before and I already knew before he introduced himself that he was your brother. We struck up a conversation about the door and he told me he had the opener but hadn't found time to install it."

She didn't respond. She just stared out the windshield with a tear tracking down her face and her lips quivering.

I caught the tear with my finger and she turned her head away. "Let me ask you a question. Did they always have an omelet on the menu named December Morning?"

Her head spun toward me again. "What are you talking about? We never named our dishes," she huffed.

I held my hand out to the side. "Well, I ordered the December Morning omelet. It reminded me a lot of you. It was beautiful and soft, but had depth to it with a little bit of spice hiding in the middle." I smiled and she snorted a little and rolled her eyes.

After a few moments, she asked another question. "Did everything on the menu have a name?"

"No, that was the only thing I saw," I admitted.

"Did the omelet have ham, mushrooms, tomatoes, pepper jack cheese, and a white hollandaise sauce?" she asked quietly and I nodded. Another tear ran down her cheek and I swiped it away quickly. "That was never on the menu before. It was what I made every Sunday morning for myself. I didn't realize they even noticed."

I rubbed her arm soothingly. "Did you know they have a gigantic set of lips on the roof that light up?"

She dropped her chin to her chest. "You're kidding me, right?"

I laughed and shook my head. "No, I'm not kidding you. Noel told me that it has been the best marketing tool he's ever used. He also told me it was an old employee's idea. He wondered if that employee would remember."

She nodded her head, her chin quivering and her hand coming up to cover her mouth. She sat quietly with her eyes closed while tears leaked from the lids.

"He told me something else, too. He said a wise woman once told him every person you meet in the restaurant has a story. Take the time to listen to it because it might change your life. The pain in his eyes when he told me that woman was his sister was overwhelming," I whispered, rubbing her back.

She leaned her head on my shoulder and sobbed. "I miss him so much. It's like half of me is dead, and I don't even have a place to go and be with him. For the first seventeen years of our life, we were inseparable. We were twins, but we were best friends, too. I never dreamed I'd have to live my life so isolated from him."

I kissed her forehead and held her tightly. "You don't have to anymore. It was obvious to me how much he misses you. I offered to install the handicapped door opener so you two could see each other again, even if you only say two words. I know it was wrong to not include you in the decision, but I remembered you telling me you had tried to reach out to him. I was hoping if I could bring you together somehow, things might change. I understand if you aren't ready, though. Let me take you home and you can think about it. I can come down tomorrow with Dully and fix the door."

She shuddered in my arms and let out a breath. "If I go home and think about it, I'll never do it. He's rejected me too many times for my heart to withstand another."

I kissed her on the lips, her tears salty on my own. "I understand, and I'm sorry for making your heart hurt. That's not what I was trying to do."

She sat up and wiped her face, her hands still shaking. "You had good intentions, but he told me he never wanted to see me again. If I show up there unannounced, it could be ugly. What if he tells me to get out?"

"What if he doesn't?" I asked, my brow raised. "I don't know him, like at all, but after talking with him for those few minutes over breakfast, it was easy to see he regretted his angry words toward you. He wants to see you, but his pride, and his shame, is getting in the way."

She sighed and the sound was unsure and shaky. She sat up and buckled her seatbelt, her face changing from scared to resolved. "Okay, then let's go install a handicapped door opener."

I snapped my seatbelt on and put the truck in drive. I drove down the road toward Kiss's Café in silence. I was afraid if I said a word and broke the spell, she'd change her mind.

Chapter Fifteen

We were parked in front of a deserted Kiss's Café, and I turned to December. "You sure?"

She smiled weakly and nodded. "I never wanted it to be like this. I have to try one more time, but I'm glad you're with me."

"I'm glad I'm here, too. Let me get Sport." I dropped her hand and opened my door, but she was out of the truck and around, lifting it out before I could even get the remote. She set it up on the ground and waited for it to open, then held it while I transferred in. I didn't say anything. I understood she needed to do something to keep herself calm. She pushed me up and over the curb and gazed at the giant set of lips on the roof. A smile lifted her lips and she shook her head.

"I told them it would look hot. I wasn't lying," she chuckled. She reached for the door handle, but pulled back and took a deep breath. "I can do this," she whispered before she pulled it open and held the door so I could wheel through. She followed me in and then turned back to make sure it closed.

"Hey, Jay, thanks for coming," Noel said, coming out of the kitchen with a full tray of silverware.

He set it down and came over, shaking my hand. December stiffened and I waited for her to turn, but she didn't. I worried she might bolt out the door and I'd never see her again.

"Good to see you again, Noel," I said, shaking his hand.

He dropped his hand and his gaze traveled to the woman at the door. The woman still facing the street. He was curious at first and then recognition hit him. He stepped back like he'd been punched, a whoosh of air escaping from between his lips.

"December?" he asked, his voice questioning.

She turned slowly and I reached for her, taking her hand. She pulled the cap off her head and held it to her side, fisting it in her hand.

"Hi, Noel," she answered, her voice wavering a bit in the quiet café.

"What are you doing here?" he asked. His tone wasn't accusatory or angry, it was more curious with a touch of sadness.

"She's the helper I mentioned. She's my..." I was trying to decide between friend and girlfriend when she piped up.

"I'm his fiancée," she stuttered. I squeezed her hand and tried to look cool. Inside, my mind was going ninety miles an hour over bumpy terrain. Fiancée? Had she lost her mind?

"You're getting married?" Noel asked in shock.

She nodded her head vigorously. "Yes, next, um, Friday."

His brows went up. "You're getting married on

Christmas Eve?"

"All my family will be home for the holidays," I jumped in quickly.

"She's not wearing a ring," he volleyed back.

"It was too big, so the jeweler is resizing it before the ceremony."

What was I doing?

"I see. You didn't mention you were engaged to December when you were here last week, Jay," Noel said bitterly.

I grimaced but nodded, my hands held up against my chest. "I have no excuse, Noel. I mostly just wanted to see the restaurant. I had no idea you'd be here. When you spoke about your sister, I felt your pain and loneliness. I promised December it wasn't my intention to stick my nose in where it didn't belong, but I could see how much you missed her. She misses you, too, and wishes things were different. If you don't, well, I can't change that, but please be respectful while she's here. We'll install the opener and be on our way."

She squeezed my hand, hanging on for dear life, while Noel stared at us. The war going on inside him was evident in his eyes.

Finally, he turned toward the window where the cook was watching curiously. "Nick, can you grab that door opener from the back and help Jay with it. My sister and I have some catching up to do."

Nick waved from the kitchen and disappeared from the window.

Noel turned back to us. "If you'd like to talk while Jay fixes the door, I'll get you some coffee. I have a few things to say."

I glanced at December and then back to Noel, worried that what he was going to say was going to hurt her even more, but she squeezed my hand and straightened her backbone.

"A cup of coffee sounds great." She smiled, dropped my hand, and stepped around my chair to follow Noel to the counter.

"Do you still drink it with two creams and one sugar?" he asked his tone a little friendlier.

She laughed and nodded her head. "I know, it's the girly way to do it, but that's how I still drink it."

She accepted the mug from him and they slid into a booth as Nick came out of the kitchen with the opener and the toolbox on a cart.

I shrugged out of my jacket and laid it on a stool, rubbing my hands together as he approached me. "I hope you know what you're doing, man," Nick said while I inspected the model of opener he'd brought out.

"Oh, yeah, this is the easiest one out there to install. It won't take us but a few minutes," I assured him, opening the box while I kept my eye on December and Noel.

He laughed a little and shook his head. "No, I mean with those two. They're so much alike I'm not sure either one of them will bend."

My hands paused in their work and I glanced up at him. "Do you know December?"

"Yeah, I went to school with her. She probably doesn't recognize me since I've lost a hundred pounds and gained a few years on the face. Anyway, those two were always butting heads, but they loved each other."

I pulled everything out of the box and laid it out on the cart, wishing he'd quit talking so I could hear them, but in reality, I was too far away to get anything more than a word here and there.

"Well, December has reached out to her brother multiple times over the years, but he's never accepted the olive branch. The fact they are sitting there not killing each other right now says something," I informed him pointedly.

He stuck his hands in his pockets and rocked back on his heels. "She has, huh? Well, the way he plays it, the reason they don't see each other is because she's not interested. I wondered, though. She was always the one to fix every argument that came up in the family. It didn't make a lot of sense to me."

I laid the door piston and motor on my lap and wheeled over to the door, instructing him on how to attach the motor system to the top of the door. I was grateful Noel had gotten the system that didn't require wiring and ran on a continuous charge system. They were fast and easy to install. I didn't want to leave her alone with Noel for too long.

While we worked, Nick told me about going to school with the twins and how this place was their

Friday night hang out, and their Sunday afternoon study hall. He was a year younger than them, but had a secret crush on December until she up and left town, and he never saw her again. He was working to buy this café from Noel, so Noel could move on and open the next one. It seemed Noel was having a hard time letting go of this one, though.

I enjoyed listening to his stories, but my heart was only half in it. The other half was thinking about why December would tell her brother we were engaged.

Did she think beginning a reconciliation with a lie was going to help matters? Was she just nervous and didn't know what to say? Did she feel like she needed to prove that she had made something of herself? My mind was spinning, wondering if she really wanted to marry me or if I was just a convenient story to tell her brother. I would marry her in a heartbeat if I thought it was what she really wanted, but we'd only been together a month. She needed more than a month, right?

"What's next? Jay?" Nick asked and I glanced up at him, shaking my head a little.

"Sorry, um, we just have to install the plates for the door openers, and test it out."

I explained how to install the plates and he took one outside while I attached the inside one. I screwed in the plate and reassembled the unit, snapping the handicapped symbol over the top to complete it. Nick motioned to me and I nodded. He hit his button and the door slowly opened until it stopped just short of the wall. He stepped through and within seconds, it was closing again. I did the same with my button on the inside and was happy to see the door responded perfectly.

Nick picked up the screwdrivers and wrenches and laid them back in the box. "If I'd a known it was that easy, I would have installed that weeks ago."

I shrugged. "They can be intimidating for most people. We lucked out that Noel got the easy system. It's not cheap, but it's the best, in my opinion. Easy to install, easy maintenance, and, most importantly, happy customers."

"Well, we appreciate you coming over to help us with it. Have you and December eaten? I can go whip something up," he offered.

I glanced over at them at the booth. They both had tears on their faces, but their hands were joined in the middle of the table.

"That would be great, Nick. Give us about ten minutes and then start two December Mornings," I said, never taking my eyes off the woman who just might be my every morning.

KISS

"Hi, I know it's late, but do you have two rooms available?" I asked the clerk at the hotel.

She did some typing into the computer and looked up. "No, I'm sorry. I only have one room left and it has a king-size bed. It is handicapped accessible. Will that work?" she asked, glancing between December and me.

"That would be perfect," December answered, sliding her card across the counter. "We'll take it."

I sat quietly and waited for her to fill out the paperwork and sign the check-in paper. She was absolutely wiped out and ready to drop. Even though the drive back to Snowberry was only an hour, it was snowing and already midnight. She'd convinced me a hotel would be safer than being on the road.

The clerk handed her the key and she picked up the two backpacks at my feet and slung them over her shoulder. I followed her down the hallway to the last room and stopped while she tried to get the door open. It unlocked, only to lock again when she turned the handle. She was close to tears and I reached for her hands, stilling them against the door.

"Take a deep breath, December. Let me unlock the door and then you can relax, okay?"

She nodded and I took the key, unlocking the door and holding it with my arm while she walked through, pulling it the rest of the way open for me.

The room was clean and inviting, with the quaint lamp on the bedside table lighting up the small space. She set the backpacks on the bed and gave me a tired smile. "Thanks for agreeing to stay the night. I'm too tired to deal with driving home. I sort of feel like while we're here, together in this room, nothing else matters. Like you can hold me all night long and no one will ever be the wiser."

I took both her hands in front of me and held them gently. "I understand how you're feeling. I've wanted to take you in my arms for hours, but things were going so well with Noel that I held back. Go shower and then we'll crawl into bed." I picked up her backpack and handed it to her. "Smart thinking on bringing a bag, you never know about Minnesota winters."

She took it from me and turned toward the bathroom. "Do you want to shower with me?" she asked over her shoulder.

I motioned at the chair. "I can't. It's not safe."

Her face fell and she came back over to me. "Would you rather go home? I forgot it's not easy to travel sometimes."

I turned her back to the bathroom. "No, I'm okay. I'll clean up when you're done. Just relax now, the hard part is over."

She nodded her head and breathed out a *yeah* before shutting the bathroom door. I grabbed my phone and typed out a quick text to Dully to let him know we were staying over. I know she wanted to be incognito, but I didn't want him to worry if my truck wasn't in the garage in the morning.

To my surprise, my phone dinged almost immediately with his response. *"Glad to hear you're staying safe. The snow is coming down hard here and we just got back from the ER. Sunny was burning up.*

She has a double ear infection but will be fine in the morning, I'm sure. You know how she is."

I frowned. My little girl was sick and I wasn't there. I typed back. "Kiss her for me and tell her I'll see her in the morning. Do you think she'll be able to come to the festival tomorrow night?"

I set the phone down and pulled some things out of my bag, a clean pair of sleep pants, a shirt, and my medication. The shower was running and I rolled to the sink and wet a washcloth, washing my face and hands. My phone dinged and I checked the message while I brushed my teeth.

"Like we're going to be able to keep her away? We'll make her rest all day and she'll be there, at least for a little while. Going to sleep now. Drive safe and see you in the morning."

I clicked the phone off and finished washing up, slipped my clean shirt over my head, and quickly washed my legs with the washcloth. The water in the shower shut off and I grabbed the sleep pants and pulled them on over my feet then rocked my hips until they were around my waist.

I wheeled to the bed, ready to climb in, but it was higher than most beds and getting onto it was going to be a trick. So much for a handicapped accessible room. I was still staring at it when I heard the click of the bathroom door.

"That felt great. Let me get the bed ready and we can sack…" She stopped midway through her sentence when she saw me sitting there. "Jay, is there a problem?"

"I can't figure out how to get on the bed. I'm embarrassed to admit I'm going to need help."

She leaned down and kissed me, her lips and tongue tasting of peppermint. When the kiss ended, she lowered a brow. "There is nothing embarrassing about asking for help, Jay. I'll never hesitate to help you, and I hope you won't hesitate to ask for it, either."

I sighed with relief and nodded. "It's a hard thing for me because I pride myself on my independence."

She kissed my lips again and held my eye. "I know you do, but you also know that sometimes, when you're in a situation that's unfamiliar, you will have to make some concessions, right?" She turned and pulled the comforter down to the foot of the bed, fluffing the pillows and arranging them just so. "If I grab you under your arms, can we swing you up onto the bed? You could probably pull yourself up, but I'm afraid you'll hurt your back."

"Yeah, all I need is a boost to get my butt on the bed. I only weigh one-sixty, so hopefully, I'm not too much of a lug," I joked.

"No, I'll be fine. Ready?" she asked, her tone clipped.

She didn't give me time to answer, she just tucked her hands under my armpits and lifted me up to the bed. I pushed myself back with my hands and swung my legs up on the mattress while she pulled Sport over, in case I needed it in the night.

She sat down on the bed and I pulled her over to me, rubbing her back.

"Thanks for helping me. Did I do something wrong?" I asked, kissing her neck tenderly.

"No, I'm just tired," she answered, but her body was unyielding under my fingers.

I kept massaging her shoulders and then tucked my cheek against hers. "I don't believe you."

She sighed heavily and her shoulders slumped. "You said you weigh one-sixty, and I realized I weigh more than my boyfriend does."

"Your boyfriend, huh? A few hours ago, I was your fiancée," I joked and she hung her head. I went back to rubbing her shoulders, wondering how to make her feel better after a rough day of confrontation. "For the record, I don't care how much you weigh. I'm lucky and thankful that you're beautiful and strong. I'm also glad you're mine, whether I'm your boyfriend, your fiancé, or your husband."

I lowered us to the pillows and twined our hands together to rest on her hip.

"I love you so much, Jay. Thank you for caring enough to stick your neck out and bring me here. You were right about Noel missing me. He apologized for treating me the way he has in the past. He wanted to make amends and be part of my life, but he figured he'd blown it and didn't know how to ask."

I raised our hands and kissed the back of hers. "I'm glad you can mend your relationship and be happy again. I think your Mom and Dad would be very proud of both of you tonight. I know I was. You're so beautiful, kind, and caring. I know going there wasn't easy, but I also know you didn't go for yourself, did you?"

"Of course, I did. Who else would I go there for?" she asked perplexed.

"For Noel. You had to go see for yourself if he was okay. The moment I told you he was hurting, a fleck of worry appeared in your eyes. Even though it was the hardest thing you'd ever done, there was no way you were going home without making sure he was okay. That's what I love about you. You worry about everyone else first before you worry about yourself. You've earned the right to rest tonight. I want you to do what makes you happy."

She scooted closer until she was plastered up against me, her ample chest squished nearly in my face and her leg slipped between mine. "You make me happy," she murmured, before crushing her lips against mine.

Her tongue pressed hungrily against my lips until I opened them, allowing her entrance. I rubbed her hip and pulled her even closer to me, tangling my hand in her hair when she moaned against my mouth. I trailed kisses up to her ear and then down behind it, kissing and sucking her neck until she arched against me.

"Touch me, please," she begged softly into the night.

My hand caressed her breast and she sucked in

a breath when my thumb flicked over her taut nipple. I moaned when her hand slithered between us and the heat of it burned through the sleep pants. She rubbed up and down rhythmically until I was firm in her hand. I moaned loudly, loving the way she touched me.

I kissed my way to the top of her tank top and then slid my hand underneath, pulling it back so I could see her, touch her. My lips found their way to her plump nipple, its peak a beacon for my tongue. I suckled it gently, feeling myself growing harder with each stroke of her hand.

"Make love to me, Jay. Please," she begged, pressing her chest into my mouth when I bit down on her nipple gently.

Her words slowed my suckling and I slowly pulled her shirt down over her breasts again. I cupped her cheek and held her eyes, which were still filled with lust. "I can't, sweetheart."

Her hand, still holding me, squeezed my hardness. "But..." she looked down and back up. A light came on in her eyes and she smiled. "It's okay. I'm on the pill."

I grasped her hand to stop it and held it against my chest. "Believe me, I want this just as much as you do. You're gorgeous and your body is driving me to distraction. Obviously, my body, mind, and heart think so, too, because one touch of your hand and the little issue I'd been having disappeared. I just..." I took a deep breath and held her gaze, nothing but honesty for her to see in mine.

"I won't make love to you tonight. We've waited a long time to be with the person we knew was right for us. While tonight is charged and full of emotion, I don't want you to have any regrets in the morning. We can wait another week until we're married and then I'll never stop making love to you," I promised, kissing her lips softly.

She blinked a few times and her brow quirked up at a funny angle. "Jay, obviously, we aren't really getting married next Friday. I don't know why I said that. It just came out. I couldn't even form a coherent thought standing there. We aren't even engaged."

"You invited him to the wedding, December," I teased, running my hand down her sweet face, "and he accepted."

She puffed up her cheeks and then let them deflate again. "Don't worry, I'll just tell him we changed our minds and decided to wait. It's Christmas Eve, I'm sure he will find other plans."

I picked up her hand and kissed her palm, helping her to turn over and snugging her bottom against me.

"Do you want to go to Snowberry Fest with me tomorrow night?" I asked, changing the subject.

"Of course, this will be my first, but I've heard all about it," she said excitedly even through the fatigue in her voice.

"I have to play from seven to eight, but after that, I'm all yours." I kissed her neck and she rubbed my hand resting on her belly.

"Play? Play what?" she asked, confused.

I laughed and kissed her neck again. "I play mandolin. Didn't you know that?"

She flipped over and shook her head. "No, I didn't know that. Did you know I play the guitar?"

I laughed even harder. "No, I didn't know that. Do you sing?"

"Can't carry a tune in a bucket." She gigglesnorted and I tickled her until she did it again because I loved the sound of it.

"Maybe we should make this the December Kiss show then? We'll play together, Sunny and I will sing, and at the end, we'll kiss under the mistletoe?" I teased, plunking a kiss on her nose.

Her eyes were almost closed, but she smiled from ear-to-ear. "Mmm, sounds perfect."

She drifted off to sleep as a plan came together in my mind. The more I thought about it, the more certain I was it had to happen. I was going to need everyone's help to pull it off, but if I did, this would be a Christmas she would never forget.

I ran my hand along her face tenderly and she smiled in her sleep. "My Christmas has come early, pretty lady, and I'm going to make sure yours does, too."

Chapter Sixteen

I grabbed a Diet Coke from the fridge and popped the top, taking a swig of the sweet bubbles. The clock read eleven a.m., which meant I only had a few hours to get everything in order for tonight. I set the can on my table and rolled to the bedroom, dropping my dirty clothes in the laundry room on the way by.

There was a knock on the door. "Yeah, come in!" I called, knowing it was probably Sunny. Dully had texted me this morning that she was feeling better already.

The door opened and my little sunshine skipped through the door, followed by her Mom and Dad.

"Well, well, the gangs all here," I teased when Snow closed the door behind them.

"We're dying to hear about the calendar shots," Snow admitted, hanging their coats on the rack.

I motioned Sunny over to me and she climbed up on my lap. "I can do better than that. I can show them to you."

Snow and Dully both grinned and Sunny laid her head on my chest. "I missed you, Uncle Jay. I had to go to the hospital without you. Miss December wasn't even there."

I hugged her little warm body against me. "I'm sorry, baby. I was with Miss December in Rochester. I'm glad you're okay."

She patted my cheeks with her tiny hands. "Today, my ears are all fine," she promised, holding her hands up and shrugging. "What did you and Miss December do?"

I rolled my chair forward and winked at Dully and Snow. "We went to pick up the pictures for the hospital calendar. I've seen them, and I know we're going to sell lots and lots of calendars for the playground." I tickled her belly and she belly laughed until her father swooped her off my lap, so I could get the proofs out of my bag.

Snow glanced around the cabin. "Where is December?"

"I dropped her off at home a few hours ago. She wanted some time to tune her guitar and bone up on her Christmas carols before tonight."

"Her guitar?" Dully asked, surprised.

"I know, right? I was as surprised as you are. I invited her to play for the hour with me in the bandstand on the condition she doesn't have to sing."

"I can sing, Uncle Jay!" Sunny clapped and I blew her a kiss that she went chasing after.

"How are you feeling, Snow?" I asked my sister-in-law while I dug in my bag.

"I'm feeling great. I saw Dr. Montag and he

said our little miracle is perfect. Nothing to worry about."

"I do worry. I mean, you passed out. Why do they think that happened?" I asked, my voice concerned even though I tried to be cool.

"They did some blood tests and I'm anemic. Also, my blood sugar was low when they got me to the ER that day. I'm on iron and making sure I eat small meals more frequently. You worry too much, but I love you for it." She pointed at my bag. "Come on with those already. I'm dying here."

I laid the proofs out on the table in order of the months of the year. Dully and Snow stared at them for the longest time without saying a word.

"These are incredible," Snow finally said, tears in her eyes.

"I think so, too. Noble sent them to the board president via email. We've asked them to approve them quickly, so we can send them to the printer. We won't have them for Snowberry Fest, but we will have them by next week for the Christmas tea at the hospital. That was the best I could do," I apologized, stacking them up again.

"Best you could do? Jay, a calendar wasn't even going to happen this year before you stepped in. You've pulled off a Christmas miracle. Is Newman's Printing going to run them?" Snow asked.

"Nope. I got a phone call from a printer across the border in Wisconsin. They heard about the project and have offered to print a thousand copies for us, free of charge. That's what we've sold in the past, so I figured it was a good place to start," I explained.

"But, Jay, why? A thousand calendars will be a lot of money for a small printer," Dully exclaimed.

"Their daughter is seven and suffers from muscular dystrophy. When they heard what the proceeds were going to be used for, they wanted to help. They said they would drive the thirty miles to Snowberry just so their daughter finally had a place to play. I think that says it all right there."

Dully nodded with a smile on his face. "And then some. I'm proud of you, Jay. You've really pulled this together quickly and professionally. Those photos tell me we'll probably sell way more than a thousand, though."

I patted the table with my hand. "If we do, I'll work with the printer and have more printed. If we sell a thousand of them, we'll have twenty thousand dollars and the playground is a reality. Anything over and above that is gravy."

"Uncle Jay, what's this?" Sunny's little voice asked from the living room and we all swung around to see her holding a black box.

Dully walked over to her and squatted down next to her, holding his hand out for the box. "Yeah, Uncle Jay, what's this?"

I glanced at Snow and rolled my eyes a little. She giggled and shook her head at me, but threw me a wink of encouragement.

"That, my dear brother, is an engagement ring. Have you ever seen one before? Gold and diamonds? They sparkle?"

Snow snorted and Dully tossed it up in the air and caught it before tossing it to me, where I grabbed at it quickly. "Could you not? This wasn't cheap!"

Dully grinned and laughed in a way I hadn't heard him laugh in a long while. "I don't imagine it was. How come I didn't know anything about this?"

"It was a last-minute thing?" I asked, hoping that would be enough of an explanation for them.

Snow laughed. "Yeah, like that's going to fly. Spill it."

I sighed and set the ring on the table. "December and I went to see her brother last night at the café. When we first got there, she introduced me as her fiancé and told him we're getting married next Friday."

Snow shook her head in confusion. "Next Friday is Christmas Eve."

"I don't think she was thinking clearly, Snow. When all was said and done, she and Noel patched things up, but now he thinks he's coming to our wedding next week."

Dully plunked down on the couch. "But you aren't even engaged."

I tapped the ring box. "Yet. I hope to change that tonight."

Snow waved her hand around in the air. "Wait, wait, so you're going to propose to a girl, and marry her, just so she can save face with her brother?"

I stared at my brother and sister-in-law for a moment and shook my head slowly. "No, I'm going to propose to a girl and marry her because I love her. If I'm lucky and she says yes, and I'm kind of thinking she's going to, I'm going to love her forever for the kind and beautiful soul that she is. Last night, after we left the café, she said she didn't know what she was thinking telling him that, but I didn't have to marry her. Last night, watching her sleep, there was nothing I wanted more. We haven't been together long, and I know this will be a shock for everyone, but she makes me happy. Happier than I've ever been. I was hoping you'd be happy for us, too, or at least respect my decision to make December part of our family."

Sunny climbed up on my lap and pulled the box open, staring at the shiny diamond. "I respect your decision, my little Jaybird. I like Miss December. I hope she says yes, but if she does, you have to promise you'll seal it with a kiss." She held up her finger to my lips and I kissed it, making a smawk sound as she pulled it away.

"Sunny, can you run up to the house and wait for Grandma, then bring her down here? She's on her way, but don't tell her about Uncle Jay's surprise," Dully whispered and Sunny beamed as she climbed down off my lap.

"Yes, Daddy, I'll be right back." She grabbed her coat and bounced out the door and down the ramp.

"Why is mom on her way?" I asked, glancing

between them.

"Because if we're going to plan a wedding in a week, we're going to need all the help we can get," Dully answered.

Snow laughed and clapped her hands excitedly. "I wasn't being disrespectful, Jay, I was making sure you were doing this for the right reasons. I have no doubt now."

Dully grasped his wife's shoulders and held my eye. "When I proposed to Snow, I'd known her about the same amount of time you've known December. I understand the way you're feeling right now. Don't worry, your family is behind you. We'd be proud to call December an Alexander. Leave everything to us, all you need to worry about is making sure she says yes."

I shook the ring at him. "I don't think that's going to be a problem."

KISS

My hands were sweating as I strummed the last chord of Silent Night. Sunny wasn't feeling well enough to sing, so she sat on Dully's lap in the audience and listened quietly to us play the requests from the audience. The bandstand was surprisingly warm, and everyone was happy to sing along to their favorite carols.

We only had time for one more song and I leaned into the microphone, catching Dully's eye. He gave me a thumbs up and I turned my head toward December while still addressing the crowd.

"Thanks for coming out to Snowberry Fest tonight. I've written a special song to end the show, and I hope you enjoy it."

December glanced at me questioningly and I leaned back in Sport and winked. "This one's for you, sweetheart," I whispered so only she could hear.

"December Kiss, how beautiful is she?
More beautiful than a December morning breeze. A December kiss on a Christmas night is all I've ever dreamed. We'll meet under the mistletoe and dance our fears away. I never expected to feel this way. I never expected to need you this way. Now can I, now will you, let me steal you away? My love. My life. Listen to my promises this night. How beautiful is she? I just can't wait to see her shining eyes under the mistletoe with me."

I finished the last chord and the bandshell was so quiet you could hear a pin drop. I set my mandolin in the stand next to me and flipped a switch on Sport until it tipped forward and started to fold, with me still in it.

December frantically reached out to help just as the chair stopped, with me almost on my knees on the floor. I took December's hand and my eye caught Sunny standing by the stage, her little hands grasping the top of it.

"You can do it, my little Jaybird," she whispered.

I gave her a little wink and the audience all

cooed and awed at her sweetness.

December was staring at me in complete shock and I squeezed her hands in mine. "We made a few modifications to the chair this afternoon because I wanted to do this right. I'm not sure how much time we have before it collapses, so Snow suggested I make this quick," I joked and the audience chuckled while December sat across from me looking concerned.

I kissed her hand and mouthed, *just kidding*.

"This is the closest I could get to being on one knee in front of you today. I knew you'd understand if I did nothing more than sit in my chair and ask you to marry me, but I wanted to show you I'll always go that extra mile. I'll always find a way to return the love and support you give me. I might not be able to do things the same way most guys do, but I'll never stop trying to show you how much I love you. We won't run down the aisle after we're married while our friends and family cheer, but I do promise not to roll over your toes." She laughed even though tears were already falling down her cheeks. "I won't be able to sweep you into my arms and carry you across the threshold, but I will give you a ride. What I'm trying to say is, I'll always find a way to give you the same experiences every other woman has in life, because I love you that much. I used to lie in bed at night and wonder what this life had planned for me, but I never found the answer. Then one warm November afternoon, my whole life changed. December, I know we haven't known each other long, but I've loved you since the day you were born, it just took me this long to find you." I pulled a ring box off the piece of Velcro next to my leg and opened it. "December, will you give me the honor of being the one to kiss you awake every morning? Will you marry me?" I asked, hope in my heart and a smile on my face.

Her face was wet, and her hands were shaking. "Are you sure?" she squeaked. "I was just kidding last night."

The audience chuckled and Sunny jumped up and down until she couldn't stand it any longer and ran up the stairs. She whispered something in December's ear whose chin quivered a little. Finally, Dully pulled Sunny off the stage.

"Yes, sweetheart, I've never been this sure of anything in my life," I whispered. "I promised you'd only have to wait a week, and I intend to keep that promise."

She smiled then and finally answered my question. "Yes, Jason Alexander, I will marry you."

I pushed the button to straighten the chair while the audience stood, clapping and cheering. I slipped the ring on her finger and pulled her onto my lap for a kiss.

The audience was so loud no one could hear us, so I whispered in her ear. "Look, it's a perfect fit. I love you, December."

She didn't answer me, just turned her head and kissed me with her whole heart.

Chapter Seventeen

December

"Yes, okay, thank you, Teresa. I'll be in tomorrow at ten then," I paused while my boss, and friend, on the other end of the line, jabbered excitedly. I laughed at her silliness and shook my head. "Tell me about it! Having Jay propose to me in front of the whole city was not what I was expecting. As far as getting married on Christmas Eve, that's a long story, but I'll tell you tomorrow between patients. See you then."

She made me promise two more times to give her the whole story before she'd hang up. Teresa had changed the schedule so I could work Tuesday and Wednesday, and then have the holidays off. I wasn't scheduled to work Christmas Eve or Christmas day anyway, but I would make sure to send a big fruit and cheese tray to my colleagues who were working on Christmas Day. I set the phone down, still chuckling.

Yesterday morning, I got a call from Savannah and she asked me to come down to her shop. When I got there, Snow was waiting with coffee and together they showed me all the ideas they'd come up with the night before. I was in shock thinking about how many flowers she had planned for this simple ceremony. Savannah told me flowers were a symbol of life, and on Christmas Eve, they were a symbol of hope and promise.

She picked a simple purple-tinged narcissus for mine and Snow's bouquets, with matching boutonnières for the men. Sunny would skip down the aisle throwing white rose petals like snow-flakes, and the front of the chapel would be done in poinsettias, which were already there for the Christmas Eve service. I was hard-pressed to find anything I didn't like about their plans. They beamed with pride and Savannah finalized the orders, promising she'd have it all to the chapel by Friday afternoon.

Getting married on Christmas Eve may not have been the best idea I'd ever had. All of the chap-els and churches had services planned, and most restaurants were closed. After a few phone calls, Snow had arranged for our ceremony to take place in the hospital chapel between the two Christmas Eve services. It was too much to expect people to give up time with their family on Christmas Eve to attend a wedding reception, so we would throw one of those after the first of the year. It didn't much matter to me, I wasn't getting married for the party. I was getting married because I wanted nothing more than to be with the man I loved.

We had just shut down Savannah's computer and were ready to head to the dress shop when

Savannah nearly collapsed, writhing in pain. Her face was contorted in a spasm, and tears leaked from her eyes. Snow helped her breathe through the pain and after what seemed like forever, her face relaxed and she lay exhausted on Snow's lap.

Snow checked her pupils quickly and then made a phone call that ended in us taking Savannah to the emergency room. Savannah had fussed about going, insisting she couldn't afford a doctor and it wasn't that bad. I haven't known Snow very long, but the look she shot her was enough to make me fall into line, and I wasn't the one with the problem.

I made a mental note to check on Savannah before I went to the dress shop to find something to wear for my wedding day. I didn't want a big dress with a long train. I wanted simple, elegant, and preferably white, considering, as tradition goes, I'm one of the few in this day and age who could wear it. I hadn't closed my mind off to other things, though, and hoped I could find something that fit, as I didn't have time for alterations.

I blew out a breath. That seemed like a tall order even to me, but I grabbed my coat and stuck one arm in the sleeve. I was reaching for the other when the doorbell rang. I wasn't expecting any deliveries, but I shrugged my coat on and went to the door. I peeked through the window and was shocked to see who stood on my doorstep. I pulled the door open quickly.

"Noel, what are you doing here?" I asked my

brother, who stood on my porch with a gigantic box in his arms.

"Hi. Um, I wanted to bring you something." He indicated the box in his hands and I held the door, motioning for him to come in.

He swung the box through the screen door and set it on the couch, turning and wiping his hands on his pants. "I should have called first. You're busy."

I glanced down at my coat as I shut the door. "No, no, I was just running out to do some errands. I have time," I assured him, shrugging out of my coat. "Do you want some coffee?"

"Coffee, yes, coffee would be good," he stuttered, and I stared at him, puzzled.

"Noel, I'm not going to bite. Take your coat off and sit," I encouraged him.

I watched him from the corner of my eye while I made the coffee. He sat on the couch and rubbed his hands on his pants, his eyes focused on the box perched on the table. I thought back to our Friday night discussion, and how I'd given him my contact information and encouraged him to stop by anytime. I wasn't expecting to see him already, but I was pleased he had come. The last eight years without my twin had been painfully lonely, and I would do everything in my power to be close to him again. It was as if he was searching for a place in this world, and I wanted to be there for him.

I carried the coffee back to the couch and handed him a mug then sat next to him.

"It's nice to see you again, Noel. I've missed you." I smiled, taking a sip of my coffee. He nodded and did the same, his nerves eased a little by my words.

He lowered his cup from his lips and pointed at my hand. "You got your ring back. It's beautiful. Jay has great taste in jewelry and women."

I set my mug down and twisted the diamond solitaire on my finger. I had to come clean with him about the lie I'd told Friday night, but before I could, he spoke again.

"December, are you sure Jay's the one? I mean, have you thought this out? He's in a wheelchair," he said suddenly, his voice strong, but quiet.

My gut reaction was to be angry with him for even questioning that I couldn't be head over heels in love with Jay just because he was in a wheelchair. I forced myself to take a deep breath and look at things from his point of view.

"Yes, I'm sure Jay's the one. Yes, I've thought this out. I know things won't always be easy, but that doesn't matter to me. His legs may not work, but his heart is big enough that it just doesn't matter. He's bigger than life, Noel, and I get to be part of that in the best possible way. Can I tell you something, and will you promise not to get mad?" I asked, swallowing nervously.

He sighed and nodded. "As long as you promise not to get mad when you see what's in the box."

I lifted a brow but nodded my agreement. "The truth is, Friday night when I told you Jay and I were engaged, we weren't. This ring wasn't at the jewelers being resized. It was at the jewelers, still in the display case."

"I'm confused," he admitted, his brow furrowed.

"Me too?" I questioned, laughing a little. "I don't know why I told you we were engaged, and I don't know why Jay went along with it. I told him later that night we obviously weren't getting married and that I'd come clean with you about it."

"But you're wearing a ring now?"

I held my finger up and wiggled it. "It turns out Jay went along with it because he had every intention of marrying me. He proposed Saturday night at Snowberry Fest, even getting down on one knee."

Noel was completely confused, so I handed him my phone, playing the video Snow had taken of his proposal that night. When the video finished, he had a huge smile on his face and he gave me a tight hug.

"I think he loves you." He laughed and I nodded, my heart happy that he wasn't upset I had lied to him.

"He does love me."

He pointed at my phone. "What did that little girl whisper in your ear?"

I smiled, remembering the moment that cemented everything back together in my heart. "That little girl is Jay's niece, Sunny. They're best buds. I was at his house on the anniversary of

Mom's death. She stopped by and noticed I'd been crying, so I explained why." I shook the phone. "She whispered in my ear that I should say yes because my mom would be happy in heaven if I was happy again."

He put his hand to his chest in surprise. "Intuitive little girl, eh?"

I laughed and nodded, fighting back tears. "Like you don't know. She was right, though. Mom would want us to be happy here. For the record, I was going to say yes anyway." I paused and glanced up at him. "Hey, we can postpone the wedding now that you know."

He shrugged a little but the smile never wavered from his lips. "If I had a choice, I'd get married on Christmas Eve."

"Really?" I asked, surprised, and he nodded.

"Seems like the absolutely perfect time to get married to me. Christmas is about new life, right?" he asked and I nodded. "And marriage is about starting a new life." I nodded again and he grinned. "So, Christmas Eve it is?"

I smiled, loving how even after eight years, we were still so attuned to each other. "Christmas Eve it is. Okay, so now that I've come clean, what's in the box? It's killing me to know."

He rested his hand on it for a second and then pulled it away. "Open it. I hope it's not too late."

I took the top off the box and parted the tissue paper. Inside was a dress, a very old dress. I glanced from him to the box and back to him where he rubbed his temple.

"It's Grandma Lucy's wedding dress, the same one Mom wore at her wedding," he explained. "When I moved into the house after the funeral, I found it in Mom's cedar chest. I was so angry with you, which you didn't deserve, that I couldn't bring myself to call you and offer it to you. I also couldn't bring myself to get rid of it, so I had it preserved and put it away. I forgot all about it until you showed up at the café and told me you were getting married. I wanted to give you the chance to wear it, but only if you want to."

I pulled the gown up out of the paper, the simple bead and lace pattern elegant, and typical for the World War II era. The gown was floor length and had a small jacket wrap that went over the dress. It wasn't white, rather a soft cream, much like the color of old paper. Other than the color, it was exactly what I had in mind when I pictured the gown I'd wear to marry Jay.

I lowered it back to the box and stared down at him. "I was just leaving to find a dress when you rang the bell, but I guess it came to me." He stood and I hugged him, his long arms encircling me and holding me tightly. "You and Mom were practically twins. I think it will fit you perfectly."

How nice it felt to be in his arms again. I nodded my head against his chest and pulled back a little, so I could make eye contact.

"Noel, would you walk me down the aisle Friday and be the one to give me to Jay?" I asked, my voice not as steady as I would have liked.

"Nothing would make me happier, Deccy." He sighed, rubbing my back. "I'm glad I took the time to listen to a customer's story because he taught me the most important thing of all."

KISS

I swung Sport through the patio doors and onto the deck. It was nearly eleven and I was ready to go home and have my wife to myself. I just didn't have the heart to pull her away from my family. I had long ago ditched the red bowtie I'd worn to the ceremony, but I was happy I had the suit coat when the December wind blew across the deck.

December.

I grew hard just thinking about how beautiful she looked tonight. The chapel glowed in soft light from the candles that surrounded me as I sat at the front of the tiny chapel. Sunny came down the aisle, her sweet little giggles filling the room as she carefully threw white rose petals in front of her, her tiny dress bobbing with each step.

When the music changed to Ave Maria, all eyes turned to the back of the room. December stood at the end of the aisle, her arm twined through Noel's, and I stopped breathing. Dully's hand on my shoulder reminded me to force air into my lungs. She started her walk toward me and I noticed no one stood. Instead, each person she passed handed her a flower. She stood before me for a moment while Noel gave her away and then she sat next to me in a lace-covered chair.

I stared down at the band on my finger and remembered our vows to each other. In sickness and in health. To love and to honor, as long as we both shall live. I learned after the ceremony that she had requested everyone stay seated for the ceremony, including the chaplain and the wedding party. She said no law said you had to stand up to get married, but I knew in my heart she had done it for me. It was her way of showing me she would always sit beside me, and we would always be equals.

Yesterday, I'd helped her move her things into the cabin, and last night, she'd stayed in the guest room. Having her in my bed was a temptation I couldn't resist, and I wanted our first time together to be as husband and wife. I had butterflies just thinking about spending our first night together. I was comforted in knowing that neither of us had much experience, but we were ready to celebrate our love for each other, and my inabilities weren't going to keep that from happening.

A warm little body scooted up next to me and I turned to see Sunny's angelic face. "Well, hello, Sunny. It's sort of cold out here for you. I don't want those ears to get sick again," I scolded and she swung her tiny legs a few times.

"They'll be okay, Uncle Jay. Mommy said we have to be going home because Santa won't come until I'm sleeping," she said, very seriously.

I clapped my forehead with my hand. "She's right! It's almost Christmas, and little Christmas girls need to be in bed."

She shrugged her shoulder a little. "I don't think Santa can bring me what I want."

"What do you want?" I asked, surprised. She had already sent Santa her wish list a month ago.

"I really want a little sister. Boys are stinky and pick on you," she lamented.

I tried hard not to laugh at her sadness. "Oh, honey, is there a boy picking on you?"

"Jaxen Tomlin is stinky. I don't want a boy like Jaxen in my house." She frowned and crossed her arms over her chest.

"Do we need to talk to your teacher about Jaxen bothering you?" I asked, but she shook her head no.

"I already talked to Miss Waston about Jaxen. I just don't want to live with a boy."

I frowned sadly. "But I'm a boy."

She patted my leg lovingly. "You're a nice boy who loves me and gets me ice cream and takes me swimming."

I chuckled a little and hugged her, being careful of the wheelchair tire. "You know, if you have a brother, he will love you and you can take him to get ice cream and to go swimming. Santa can't bring you what you want because babies aren't really Santa's department. The baby in your mommy's tummy is already a boy or a girl and you can't change that, but do you know what you can do?" I asked and she shook her head no. "You can love it because it's your sibling and for no other reason."

"You mean just like Aunt Mandy loves all of you boys even though she's the only girl and gets tired of you always picking on her?"

This girl was too much.

I winked and patted her hand. "Exactly like that. It must be hard on Mandy sometimes not to have a sister to talk to, but do you know what she does have?"

Sunny wrinkled her nose in question. "Lots of smelly boys around?"

I laughed and shook my head, my eyes staring up at the stars for a moment. "No. She has four boys in her life who would do anything for her to make sure she was safe. She never has to worry about anyone messing with her because she can call one of us up and we'll make sure she's safe. Do you get what I mean?"

She tapped her finger on her chin. "If I have a brother, it's okay because I can still love him. He'll be little, but someday he'll be big, and can keep me safe?"

I pointed at her and nodded.

"You're a smart boy. I love you, Uncle Jay."

I kissed her tiny hand. "And I love you. Thank you for doing such a good job at the chapel to-night."

"You're welcome. Happy wedding and Merry Christmas, my little Jaybird. Will you and Miss

December come to our house tomorrow?" she begged, her hands folded in front of her.

I scooped her onto my lap and hugged her tightly for a moment. "Merry Christmas to you, my little Sunshine. We wouldn't miss spending Christmas with you, but you know what?" I asked and she shook her head no, her tired little eyes fading fast. "You can call her Aunt December now because we're married," I teased.

She laid her tired little head on my shoulder while I wheeled back through the doors. "How about Auntie Ember? I like the ring of that."

I half-snorted, half-laughed while trying not to cry at her sweetness. "Sounds perfect, sweetheart."

I handed her sleepy body off to her daddy and found my bride, hugging her brother goodbye. "I thought you'd run away, my beautiful bride," I whispered, coming up behind her, and shaking Noel's hand.

"I was just telling Noel good night. He's going to stay in town and come over in the morning since the café is closed."

"Sounds great. It's been a wonderful, beautiful, crazy day and I'd love to visit with you when things aren't so hectic."

He assured me he would be by before lunch, and I watched him make a beeline straight for Savannah, who was sitting by Snow sipping eggnog. I'd noticed he'd stayed close to her all night, especially after she had another episode with her face.

My wife pulled my thoughts away from them. "Can we go home? I've mostly been dreaming about the wonderful, beautiful, crazy night to come."

I kissed her lips when she bent down to whisper in my ear. "Me too. Let's blow this popcorn stand. We've got some love to make."

She kept hold of my hand and we left the room quietly, sneaking out the backdoor. We'd see them all in the morning, and I didn't feel the least bit guilty not announcing our departure. Now, it was our time to be together.

We followed the snowflake lights down the path that led from my parents' house to my cabin. December shivered and I glanced up, moaning at how her dress did nothing to hide how cold she was.

"Oh, we need to hurry home," I moaned, and she grinned wickedly. We reached the deck and I was too exhausted from the day to push myself up the ramp. I ordered Sport up the ramp and dug in my pocket for the key. I finally got the door open and motioned to my wife.

"Come, sit with me, Mrs. Alexander. It's threshold time." She sat on my lap, her back resting on my chest, and I rolled us through the door to our new life. "I'm so glad to be home," I sighed, turning her towards me so I could kiss her lips. "If I had to talk to one more guy about how beautiful you are, and how it's a good thing I took you off the market, or they would have, I was going to punch someone."

She laughed and tried to climb off my lap, but I held her there, rolling the chair toward our bedroom. "You're mine now, Mrs. Alexander, and you aren't going anywhere until I've had my way with you."

I rolled into the bedroom and stopped the chair so fast she almost fell off my lap. I grabbed her around the waist and we both gazed at the room before us. It had been transformed into a beautiful lovers' lair, complete with champagne and rose petals.

"I think the Alexander women had something to do with this," she sighed, lying back on the bed. I joined her and we stared up at the ceiling. Hanging over the bed was the largest cluster of mistletoe I'd ever seen.

I laughed with pure pleasure. "I think a certain Savannah Hart had everything to do with that."

"How many stops do you think she had to make to get that much mistletoe?" December pondered.

"I don't know, but that's the last thing on my mind right now. I'd hate to let all her hard work go to waste, Mrs. Alexander."

She smiled naughtily. "You know the legend of the mistletoe, right? Any couple who kisses under it on Christmas Eve will be blessed with great fertility."

"Is that so?" I asked, working her out of the coat that covered the breasts I so desperately wanted to touch. She nodded and I cupped her breast through the dress. "Wonder what happens if you make love under the mistletoe."

Her eyes rolled back in her head a little bit when I laid a kiss on her chest above her dress. "Do you think they're trying to tell us something?" she squeaked softly.

"I think they're trying to tell me to kiss you, for starters." I tugged on the zipper of her dress until the only thing holding it on were the straps over her shoulders. She sat up and the lace fell, revealing the red and green lace bra it had concealed all night. "Oh, Christmas has come early, and Santa thinks I was a very good boy," I murmured, laying my lips against the pulse thrumming in her neck.

Her head fell backward and she gave a contented *mmmm* while I worked my way to her lips. When her soft, sweet lips covered mine, they sealed my heart with a warm December Kiss.

The Snowberry Series

Snow Daze

Trapped in an elevator with a handsome stranger was the perfect meet-cute, but Dr. Snow Daze wasn't interested in being the heroine of any romance novel. A serious researcher at Providence Hospital in Snowberry, Minnesota, Snow doesn't have time for a personal life, which was exactly the way she liked it.

Dully Alexander hated elevators, until he was stuck in one with a beautiful snow angel. Intrigued by her gorgeous white hair, and her figure-hugging wheelchair, he knows he'll do anything to be her hero.

When a good old-fashioned Minnesota blizzard traps them at her apartment, he takes advantage of the crackling fire, whispered secrets on the couch, and stolen kisses in the night. Dully will stop at nothing to convince Snow she deserves her own happily ever after.

December Kiss

It's nearly Christmas in Snowberry Minnesota, but Jay Alexander is feeling anything but jolly. Stuck in the middle of town square with a flat tire on his worn-out wheelchair leaves him feeling grinchy.

December Kiss has only been in Snowberry for a few months when she happens upon this broken-down boy next door. His sandy brown hair and quirky smile has her hoisting his wheelchair into the back of her four horse Cherokee.

When a December romance blooms, Jay wants to give December just one thing for Christmas, her brother. Will Jay get his December Kiss under the mistletoe Christmas Eve?

Noel's Hart

Noel Kiss is a successful businessman, but adrift in his personal life. After he reconnects with his twin sister, Noel realizes he's bored, lonely, and searching for a change. That change might be waiting for him in Snowberry, Minnesota.

Savannah Hart is known in Snowberry as 'the smile maker' in Snowberry, Minnesota. She has poured blood, sweat, and tears into her flower emporium and loves spreading cheer throughout the community. She uses those colorful petals to hide her secrets from the people of Snowberry, but there's one man who can see right through them.

On December twenty-fourth, life changes for both Noel and Savannah. He finds a reason for change, and she finds the answer to a prayer. Desperate for relief, Savannah accepts Noel's crazy proposal, telling herself it will be easy to say goodbye when the time comes, but she's fooling no one.

Noel has until Valentine's Day to convince Savannah his arms are the shelter she's been yearning for. If he can't, the only thing he'll be holding on February 14th is a broken heart.

April Melody

April Melody loved her job as bookkeeper and hostess of Kiss's Café in Snowberry, Minnesota. What she didn't love was having to hide who she was on the inside, because of what people saw on the outside. April may not be able to hear them, but she could read the lies on their lips.

Martin Crow owns Crow's Hair and Nails, an upscale salon in the middle of bustling Snowberry. Crow hid from the world in the tiny town, and focused on helping women find their inner goddess. What he wasn't expecting to find was one of Snowberry's goddesses standing outside his apartment door.

Drawn together by their love of music, April and Crow discover guilt and hatred will steal their future. Together they learn to let love and forgiveness be the melody and harmony in their hearts.

Liberty Belle

Main Street is bustling in Snowberry, Minnesota, and nobody knows that better than the owner of the iconic bakery, the Liberty Belle. Handed the key to her namesake at barely twenty-one, Liberty has worked day and night to keep her parents' legacy alive. Now, three years later, she's a hotter mess than the batch of pies baking in her industrial-sized oven.

Photographer Bram Alexander has had his viewfinder focused on the heart of one woman since returning to Snowberry. For the last three years she's kept him at arm's length, but all bets are off when he finds her injured and alone on the bakery floor.

Liberty found falling in love with Bram easy, but convincing her tattered heart to trust him was much harder. Armed with small town determination and a heart of gold, Bram shows Liberty frame-by-frame how learning to trust him is as easy as pie.

Wicked Winifred

Winifred Papadopoulos, Freddie to her few friends, has a reputation in Snowberry, Minnesota. Behind her back, and occasionally to her face, she's known as Wicked Winifred. Freddie uses her sharp tongue as a defense mechanism to keep people at bay. The truth is, her heart was broken beyond repair at sixteen, and she doesn't intend to get close to anyone ever again. She didn't foresee a two-minute conversation at speed dating as the catalyst to turn her life upside down.

Flynn Steele didn't like dating. He liked speed dating even less. When his business partner insisted, he reluctantly agreed, sure it would be a waste of time, until he met the Wicked Witch of the West. He might not like dating, but the woman behind the green makeup intrigued him.

A downed power pole sets off a series of events neither Flynn nor Winifred saw coming. Their masks off, and their hearts open, they have until Halloween to decide if the scars of the past will bring them together or tear them apart. Grab your broomstick and hang on tight. This is going to be a bumpy ride...

Nick S. Klaus

Nick S. Klaus is a patient man, but living next door to Mandy Alexander for five years has him running low this Christmas season. He wants nothing more than to make her his Mrs. Klaus, but she'd rather pretend he isn't real.

Mandy Alexander is a single mom and full-time teacher. She doesn't have time to date or for the entanglements it can cause. Even if she did have time, getting involved with her next-door neighbor, and co-worker, Nick S. Klaus, had disaster written all over it.

This Christmas, Nick's determined to teach Mandy that love doesn't have to be complicated, and he's got two of the cutest Christmas elves to help him get the job done. Will this be the year Santa finally gets his Mrs. Klaus under the mistletoe?

About The Author

Katie Mettner

Katie Mettner writes small-town romantic tales filled with epic love stories and happily-ever-afters. She proudly wears the title of, 'the only person to lose her leg after falling down the bunny hill,'  and loves decorating her prosthetic leg with the latest fashion trends. She lives in Northern Wisconsin with her own happily-ever-after and three mini-mes. Katie has a massive addiction to coffee and Twitter, and a lessening aversion to Pinterest — now that she's quit trying to make the things she pins.

A Note to My Readers

People with disabilities are just that—people. We are not 'differently abled' because of our disability. We all have different abilities and interests, and the fact that we may or may not have a physical or intellectual disability doesn't change that. The disabled community may have different needs, but we are productive members of society who also happen to be husbands, wives, moms, dads, sons, daughters, sisters, brothers, friends, and co-workers. People with disabilities are often disrespected and portrayed two different ways; as helpless or as heroically inspirational for doing simple, basic activities.

As a disabled author who writes disabled characters, my focus is to help people without disabilities understand the real-life disability issues we face like discrimination, limited accessibility, housing, employment opportunities, and lack of people first language. I want to change the way others see our community by writing strong characters who go after their dreams, and find their true love, without shying away from what it is like to be a person with a disability. Another way I can educate people without disabilities is to help them understand our terminology. We, as the disabled community, have worked to establish what we call People First Language. This isn't a case of being politically correct. Rather, it is a way to acknowledge and communicate with a person with a disability in a respectful way by eliminating generalizations, assumptions, and stereotypes.

As a person with disabilities, I appreciate when readers take the time to ask me what my preferred language is. Since so many have asked, I thought I would include a small sample of the people-first language we use in the disabled community. This language also applies when leaving reviews and talking about books that feature characters with disabilities. The most important thing to remember when you're talking to people with disabilities is that we are people first! If you ask us what our preferred terminology is regarding our disability, we will not only tell you, but be glad you asked! If you would like more information about people first language, you will find a disability resource guide on my website.

Instead of: He is handicapped.
Use: He is a person with a disability.

Instead of: She is differently abled.
Use: She is a person with a disability.

Instead of: He is mentally retarded.
Use: He has a developmental or intellectual disability.

Instead of: She is wheelchair-bound.
Use: She uses a wheelchair.

Instead of: He is a cripple.
Use: He has a physical disability.

Instead of: She is a midget or dwarf.
Use: She is a person of short stature or a little person.

Instead of: He is deaf and mute.
Use: He is deaf or he has a hearing disability.

Instead of: She is a normal or healthy person.
Use: She is a person without a disability.

Instead of: That is handicapped parking.
Use: That is accessible parking.

Instead of: He has overcome his disability.
Use: He is successful and productive.

Instead of: She is suffering from vision loss.
Use: She is a person who is blind or visually disabled.

Instead of: He is brain damaged.
Use: He is a person with a traumatic brain injury.

Other Books by Katie Mettner

The Fluffy Cupcake Series (2)

The Kontakt Series (2)

The Sugar Series (5)

The Northern Lights Series (4)

The Snowberry Series (7)

The Kupid's Cove Series (4)

The Magnificent Series (2)

The Bells Pass Series (5)

The Dalton Sibling Series (3)

The Raven Ranch Series (2)

The Butterfly Junction Series (2)

A Christmas at Gingerbread Falls

Someone in the Water (Paranormal)

White Sheets & Rosy Cheeks (Paranormal)

The Secrets Between Us

After Summer Ends (Lesbian Romance)

Finding Susan (Lesbian Romance)

Torched